The Bleak Horizon: A Journey Into Darkness

Declan Hunter

Published by RWG Publishing, 2023.

THE BLEAK HORIZON: A JOURNEY INTO DARKNESS

First edition. July 20, 2023.

Written by Declan Hunter.

Table of Contents

Chapter 1: The Fall of Hope: A World Unraveled

As the once thriving city of Solstice lay in ruins, the atmosphere was filled with a heavy sense of desolation. The once-soaring buildings of the city had been reduced to crumbling relics of a bygone era. The once hopeful and dreaming people now walked the streets with haunted eyes, their spirits crushed under the weight of a world that had come apart at the seams.

It started with a string of catastrophic events, like the economy collapsing, then it was followed by a string of natural disasters that were so severe that they reduced entire regions to rubble. The once-bustling metropolis resembled a ghost town now, with its empty streets serving as a spooky reminder of happier times. The fragments of lives that had been shattered could be seen strewn about like debris all over the asphalt.

Marcus Rivers, a weary survivor, trudged through the desolate landscape, and the sound of his footsteps reverberated through the void. The cityscape, which had been adorned with colorful billboards and dazzling lights in the past, now displayed messages of despair and government propaganda, which served as a constant reminder of the dystopian nightmare they were trapped in. Statue of Unity, a once-proud symbol of hope, now stood weathered and corroded, its once gleaming surface tarnished by time and neglect.

Marcus couldn't help but reflect on the good old days as he made his way through the crumbling streets. He couldn't help but think back to the time before the collapse. A universe that is brimming with possibilities and promises. Those days, however, were a distant memory; in their place stood an oppressive regime that maintained its grip on power through the use of fear and manipulation. The government, which was once looked to by its people as a reliable source of protection, had devolved into a repressive authority, enforcing stringent curfews and rationing essential resources.

As the sun descended below the horizon, an eerie light was cast over the city, and Marcus sought refuge in a building that had been abandoned. As a result of years of neglect, the walls had become discolored, and the air was thick with the odor of rot. It was a striking contrast to the home he had been accustomed to, which had been a welcoming sanctuary full of laughter and love.

Marcus could not help but think back to the day that hope had passed away as he laid down on a mattress that was falling apart. It was a day that would forever be ingrained in his mind, a day that would forever alter everything. The government had recently unveiled a brand new monitoring system, which offered assurances of increased safety and protection. But everything you saw was an act, and behind it was a thinly veiled lie. When they were first installed, the surveillance cameras were hailed as a form of protection. However, over time, they evolved into a form of control that invaded every aspect of their lives.

People started to vanish, snatched away in the middle of the night, their voices stifled for all of time. Friends, neighbors, and loved ones were gone with no trace left behind. The streets turned into a place where people whispered in fear of one another, and the only way to survive was to stay hidden and away from the watchful eyes of the regime.

Marcus's rage caused him to clench his fists, and he could feel it rising within him. He had lost everything: his family, his friends, even his freedom. He was unable to move on. But he would not allow himself to be defeated. While he was in the pit of despair, a spark of defiance ignited within him, and he made up his mind to put up a fight against the oppressive forces that were holding them captive.

Marcus solemnly committed to keeping his word to himself as the night wore on. In this dark and hopeless world, he would become a ray of light, a tinder that could light the fuse for a revolution. Together, he and the people he found who shared his views and who were unwilling to give up their humanity would bring down the structures that supported the dictatorship.

Marcus, feeling the weight of the world on his shoulders, closed his eyes, resolute to pull himself up from the ashes and reclaim the dreams that had been shattered for him and his friends. He was well aware that the journey ahead of him would be perilous, fraught with peril and uncertainty, but he also understood that he could not sit idly by as the world fell apart around him.

In the gloom, he was only able to hear one thought repeating in his head, a mantra that would serve as his compass as he made his way deeper into the unknown: "When hope dies, it is up to us to resurrect it." Because even in the darkest of horizons, there is always the possibility of a ray of hope that will bring us back from the brink. And with those words etched in his heart, Marcus drifted off into a restless sleep, ready to face the challenges that awaited him when the sun rose the following morning.

Chapter 2: Shadows of Desperation: Society on the Brink

The streets of Solstice, which were once alive with activity, are now shrouded in darkness, and the sun's feeble attempts to break through the darkened sky have been unsuccessful. At a time when society was on the verge of disintegration, despondency hung in the air like a dense mist that made it difficult to breathe.

The shattered remains of a busy marketplace that once stood in the middle of the city served as a somber reminder of times gone by when the city was in better shape. A population that was on the verge of starvation had stripped the stalls bare, leaving them empty where once they were stuffed to the brim with fresh produce and vibrant goods. The remaining merchants, who were thin and exhausted, huddled together, looking at each other with eyes that were filled with a mix of fear and longing.

One of them was a woman named Sarah Thompson, who possessed an indomitable spirit. Her worn out body reflected the cumulative effect of countless sleepless nights, as did her tattered and faded clothing. Nevertheless, in spite of the challenges she encountered, there was a glimmer of resolve in her eyes, a fire that refused to be extinguished.

Sarah had witnessed the deterioration of society and the gradual loss of compassion and empathy over the course of her lifetime. With each passing day, the government tightened its hold on the populace and instituted increasingly repressive policies in an effort to preserve its authority. Food rations were extremely limited, and those who had the audacity to speak out against the regime were met with swift and severe punishment.

Sarah couldn't help but notice the gaunt faces of her fellow citizens as she made her way through the complex maze of streets as she navigated the city. They had hollow cheeks as a result of hunger, and their strength and hope had both been sapped by it. People moved quickly as if driven by a primal instinct to survive, their eyes darting suspiciously at any sudden movement in an attempt to determine what it was.

A network of people who refused to bow down to the oppressive forces that were attempting to crush them began to come together and form a resistance in the midst of all the chaos that was occurring. They conducted their business in the shadows, keeping their activities a secret from prying eyes. Sarah had quickly established herself as a vital member of this covert organization, and her unyielding resolve fueled the group's efforts to win their freedom.

One day, as the sun was setting behind the horizon, Sarah crept into a basement that was only dimly lit. This basement served as the clandestine gathering spot for the resistance. A scattering of dissidents, all of whom wore masks and kept a low profile, gathered together. They were each burdened by the weight of their own personal tragedies, but when they banded together, they formed a formidable force that they could use to fight the growing gloom.

The charismatic figure only known by the name The Raven stood tall as he swept his penetrating gaze around the room. He was the leader of the resistance movement. In the dimly lit room, his voice could be heard carrying the weight of a rallying cry even though it was only a whisper. He talked about the importance of solidarity, resiliency, and standing together in the face of oppression as his main themes.

Sarah paid close attention while her heart raced with a mixture of fear and excitement as she listened intently. The Raven provided a rundown of their next objective, which was to infiltrate a government facility and retrieve vital information that could expose the regime's deepest, most closely guarded secrets. It was a risky mission, one that carried the possibility of being captured and executed, but they were willing to take the chance in order to complete it.

As the days turned into weeks, Sarah and her fellow comrades continued to painstakingly plan their operation. In preparation for the day that would decide their fate, they studied blueprints, planned escape routes, and worked on honing their skills. Every second that went by brought them one step closer to the edge, one step closer to the precipice of a revolution that had the potential to alter the trajectory of their hopeless existence.

As the time for the mission's nighttime assault arrived, Sarah joined the ranks of her fellow rebels, all of whom wore expressions that conveyed unwavering resolve. They moved stealthily through the darkness, keeping their steps quiet and the pounding of their hearts to themselves. They were confronted by a formidable fortress made of concrete and steel that loomed in front of them.

Sarah inhaled deeply as she took stock of her steely nerves and the blazing sense of purpose that was raging within her. She was well aware that the outcome of their mission would have far-reaching repercussions. They were no longer isolated people stumbling around in the gloom of hopelessness; rather, they had come together into a cohesive group that was prepared to reclaim their future.

As they broke through the defenses of the facility, the echoes of their footsteps reverberated through the empty corridors, serving as a spooky reminder of the society's precarious position on the edge of extinction. They were on the verge of discovering the answers they sought, and with each passing second, a surge of hope coursed through their veins, driving away the shadows of hopelessness that had been plaguing their world.

Chapter 3: Struggling Embers: A Glimmer of Resistance

The secret hideout in the basement hummed with the nervous energy of hushed conversations. A flickering ember of hope in the midst of the oppressive darkness that gripped their dystopian world could be found within the room with the dim lighting. These remnants of a resistance movement were housed within the room.

Sarah Thompson stood in front of her fellow rebels in this makeshift sanctuary, her voice calm but filled with a sense of urgency. It was time to kindle the flame of insurrection, to call on others to join their cause, and to stoke the smoldering embers of resistance into a raging blaze that would consume the repressive regime.

She told him about their most recent find, which was a cache of secret documents that detailed the government's plans for even more control and manipulation. The revelations were unsettling because they showed the extent to which their adversary had lied and manipulated them. The realization that they were in possession of this information strengthened their resolve to expose the truth and usher in a new day.

Sarah laid out their strategy while a map was spread out in front of them. It involved reaching out to communities that had been disenfranchised, rallying those who were disillusioned and oppressed, and planting the seeds of rebellion in every nook and cranny of their shattered world. It was a risky mission, one that demanded stealth, resiliency, and the utmost dedication from its participants.

As the days turned into weeks, the members of the resistance dispersed across the devastated landscape, giving each other specific missions to carry out in order to recruit new members, collect information, and disseminate the news. Sarah found herself engulfed in the center of an impoverished neighborhood called Hope's End, where the locals clung to the pieces of their shattered hopes and dreams.

The streets of Hope's End were a labyrinth of despair; there, abject poverty and utter hopelessness coexisted with the tenacity of those who refused to give up. The once bustling marketplace had been reduced to a few meager stalls, with the wares being scarce and the prices being exorbitant. The dilapidated buildings stood as monuments to broken promises, while the once bustling marketplace had been reduced to these.

Sarah made her way through the back alleys, keeping a low profile as she searched for people who were willing to stand up to the repressive regime. She had conversations with exhausted mothers and fathers who yearned for a better future for their children. She also had conversations with artists and intellectuals whose voices had been silenced by the propaganda machine that the regime had in place. The more she listened, the more she understood that their suffering had not been in vain; that their struggles were shared by an infinite number of other people.

Her words struck a chord with the people who lived in Hope's End, and a spark of defiance was ignited within each of their hearts as a result. They yearned for a change, for a chance to reclaim their dignity and emerge victorious from the ashes of their defeat. Each new member of the resistance brought with them a distinct point of view and a dogged determination to put up a fight, and the ranks of the resistance swelled with new recruits from this forgotten district over time.

Their influence on the regime increased in tandem with the resistance's growth in both numbers and strength. As rumors of discontent spread throughout the city, the government's hold on power started to become increasingly precarious. The regime's propaganda machine was having trouble maintaining control over a population that was becoming more aware of the truth, and the walls of fear and oppression were beginning to show cracks.

However, the fight was not even close to being won. In a desperate attempt to put out the ever-increasing flames of resistance, the regime reacted by increasing the amount of surveillance it conducted as well as the severity of its crackdowns. Sarah and her companions were aware that they needed to proceed with caution, as well as adapt and develop in response to each new obstacle they encountered.

Sarah convened with her allies once more in the middle of the secret hideout used by the resistance. Their spirits were tempered by the trials that they had endured, and it showed in the look that was a mix of weariness and determination in their eyes. However, the flame of insurrection burned brighter than it ever had before, defiantly refusing to be extinguished despite the brutality of the regime.

They reaffirmed their commitment to stand united against the forces of oppression and to keep the flame of resistance alive with their resolute voices. When Sarah looked into the faces of her comrades in the rebellion, she realized that their fight was not yet over. The road that lay in front of them was perilous and fraught with unpredictability, but by working together, they would create a new road—a road leading to freedom and redemption.

Sarah paused for a moment of introspection before they dispersed to carry on with their mission. She had seen the dawning of a glimmer of hope during the fight against the darkness, a guiding light that led them through the darkest of times. The embers of resistance that burned within their hearts held the promise of a better future, and she was determined to fan those embers into a roaring fire that would illuminate the path to their liberation.

Chapter 4: Ruins of Civilization: A Bleak Reminder

The desolate reality that had recently swallowed up what was left of humanity stood in stark contrast to the solemn reminders provided by the ruins of civilization, which stood as solemn reminders of a world that had once flourished. Sarah Thompson stood and observed the deteriorating buildings while feelings of awe and melancholy swelled up inside of her.

She stood on the outskirts of what had been the thriving core of Solstice, a city that had once been a guiding light toward advancement and prosperity. It lay in ruins at this time, with its once-majestic buildings reduced to skeletal frames and its streets taken over by nature's reclamation.

The once pristine architecture of the city now stood as an eerie witness to the irreversible consequences of mankind's arrogance and lack of foresight. Broken glass sparkled like shards of lost dreams, twisted metal protruded like accusing fingers, and nature crept its way through the cracks, slowly but surely reclaiming what had been taken from it.

Sarah moved cautiously through the debris, her senses being assaulted by the putrid odor of decay as well as the eerie silence that hung heavily in the air. The burden of the past pressed down upon her shoulders, prompting her to reflect on the group's ineptitude that was responsible for bringing them to this barren landscape.

She moved deeper into the ruins, and as she did so, memories began to flood her mind. These memories included images of busy streets, laughter that echoed through the alleyways, and the vibrant energy that once pulsed through the veins of the city. It was a striking contrast to the desolation that now surrounded her, and it served as a constant reminder of the price that they had paid as a result of their complacency.

The ruins also held untold tales and the secrets of a world that has been lost to the passage of time. The echo of Sarah's footsteps could be heard as she walked through the deserted hallways, and her heart was racing with a mixture of fear and curiosity. She walked into a library that had fallen into disrepair, its shelves empty, and its books reduced to ashes or pieces of paper scattered across the floor.

Sarah discovered a diary amidst the wreckage of the building, which was a remnant of the past that had been able to withstand the ravages of time. She discovered the writings of a long-forgotten author as she carefully turned the yellowed pages of the book. The diary described a society that once had faith in itself and its capabilities, as well as hope and dreams for the future. It was a stark reminder of what had been lost, a testimony to the resiliency that once resided within the hearts of the people, and it served as a stark reminder of what had been lost.

Sarah was propelled by a combination of melancholy and resoluteness when she came to the realization that they could not permit their world to become a mere footnote in history. The ruins served as a grim reminder of the price that had to be paid for allowing power to become corrupted and decay to take hold. They were a testament to the consequences of complacency.

She drew in a long breath and inhaled deeply, taking in the musty odor of discarded hopes and long-forgotten information. She heard a call to rebuild, to rise from the ashes, and to forge a new path forward as she wandered through the ruins of the once-great civilization. Sarah was well aware that the struggle they were engaged in was not only directed against the repressive regime, but also against the general apathy that had led to the disintegration of their world.

After she had finished her work in the library, Sarah emerged back into the fresh air as she looked around at the barren landscape. She saw potential in the ruins, a blank canvas upon which a new civilization could be built. They had the ability to rewrite their own history, to gain wisdom from their mistakes, and to start over with compassion, justice, and resiliency.

Sarah went back over her past actions with renewed tenacity, her mind racing with ideas for a brighter and more successful future. She was well aware that the path that lay ahead of them would be difficult and that the ruins would serve as a constant reminder of the obstacles that they would need to overcome. But despite the hopelessness of the situation, Sarah and the other people who survived steadfastly refused to give in to despair.

As she made her way back to the hideout of the resistance, she carried the weight of the ruins with her. She carried with her their stories, their failures, and the lessons they had taught. It was a burden that she gladly accepted because within it were the seeds of a new beginning. It was an opportunity to rebuild not only their physical world but also the very foundations of their society. She knew that she had to take advantage of this opportunity.

Their struggle for redemption and a better future would take place against the gloomy backdrop of the ruins of their civilization, which would serve as a constant reminder of their past.

Chapter 5: Echoes of Tyranny: The Iron Fist Tightens

As the repressive government of Solstice tightened its hold on the shattered remains of society, the reverberations of tyranny could be heard echoing through the city's broken streets. Sarah Thompson was acutely aware of the oppression that they were subjected to, as well as the oppressive presence of control and fear that pervaded every nook and cranny of their dystopian world.

Life had turned into a dangerous dance because of the iron fist of the regime, with every step being watched and analyzed by the government. The city was covered with surveillance cameras that acted as watchful eyes, recording every movement, every whispered conversation, and every act of defiance. The propaganda machine of the regime worked nonstop, spreading lies and distorting the truth in order to mold public opinion in accordance with the regime's preferred course of action.

Sarah navigated the city with extreme caution while her heart raced with a feeling that was a cross between rage and fear. The only sound that could be heard in the streets was the sound of boots slapping against the concrete, which served as a constant reminder of the presence of the regime's enforcers. The streets were filled with a heavy silence.

As Sarah made her way through the maze of alleyways, she came across instances of oppression that caused her to feel her blood begin to boil. Innocent citizens were subjected to harassment, and their rights were violated without consequence. The regime's ruthless repression machinery succeeded in silencing the voices of the dissidents who had vanished.

Any semblance of freedom and individuality was suffocated as the iron fist of tyranny tightened its hold, squeezing the life out of it. The influence of the regime extended beyond the realm of the physical, penetrating the minds of the people and manipulating their thoughts and desires in this way. Those who had the audacity to put up a fight against the oppressive regime were swiftly dealt with and had their lives cut short without any feelings of remorse. They were called traitors and considered potential dangers to the regime's hold on power.

Sarah was aware that putting up a physical fight against this oppression would not be enough to win the battle against it. It would require an unyielding defiance of the human spirit, a refusal to be broken or silenced, in order to accomplish this goal. It would require the oppressed people to have their eyes opened and their hearts filled with hope before this could be accomplished.

Sarah and the other members of the resistance gathered inside the hideout, and you could see the resolve in each of their eyes. Their hearts were filled with the reverberations of tyranny, which strengthened their determination to bring down the oppressive apparatus of the regime.

They discussed strategies to bring to the attention of the general populace the atrocities committed by the regime and to bring to the surface the truth that was buried under layers of propaganda. They devised plans for evading the surveillance network and spreading information that would shake people out of their lethargy-induced slumber. Their goal was to rouse the general population.

However, they were well aware that the dangers they faced were enormous. The reach of the regime was extensive, and its power was formidable. It had eyes and ears in every nook and cranny, and it was prepared to stifle any hint of discord. Every new day brought a tightening of the iron fist, which extinguished the tiniest glimmer of hope that had the audacity to appear.

As Sarah headed back out into the city after being inside for a while, her mind was a whirlwind of conflicting emotions: fear and determination. She was present during the regime's use of coercive methods, such as raids on the hiding places of dissidents, arbitrary arrests, and public executions, all of which were intended to strike fear into the hearts of those people who still clung to their humanity.

But even in the face of such brutality, she was able to witness acts of resistance, such as whispered conversations in dark corners, secret meetings held under the cover of night, and covert operations designed to disrupt the machinery of the regime. Even though the iron fist was tightening its grip, the embers of rebellion continued to burn brightly.

Sarah was aware that their battle would be a protracted and challenging one. The regime had no intention of giving up power without a fight. The reverberations of oppression would continue to follow them at every turn, serving as a constant reminder of the risks that were involved.

Sarah, on the other hand, experienced a revitalized sense of purpose when she met the gaze of her fellow rebels, whose eyes were filled with defiance and hope. It is possible that the iron fist will become tighter, but they will not be crushed. They would put up a fight, they would put up a resistance, and they would be the echoes of change that would reverberate all over the world they lived in.

Chapter 6: Into the Abyss: Descent into the Underbelly

The seedy underbelly of the city beckoned to me like a pitch-black abyss; it was a land of illicit dealings and undiscovered realities. Sarah Thompson stood on the edge of the cliff, getting ready to make the perilous descent into the depths of their dystopian world, which were said to hold secrets and dangers that could rip the very fabric of their society apart.

Sarah set out on her journey into the unknown armed with a sense of purpose and the determination to accomplish what she set out to do. The seedier parts of the city were like a maze, with dimly lit corridors, hidden passages, and covert gathering places tucked away everywhere. It was a world that was untainted by the watchful eye of the regime, and it was a haven for those who sought refuge from the iron fist of oppression.

As Sarah proceeded further into the forest, she could feel the growing tension in the air. The darkness was filled with murmured conversations and the exchange of whispered confidences. The underbelly consisted of a covert network, a labyrinth of rebels, criminals, and survivors who had fashioned their own existence below the radar of the regime.

Sarah went looking for assistance from a shadowy anti-government organization known as the Black Hand. They resisted the authoritarian regime by operating covertly, relying on their shady connections and their knowledge of the system's inner workings. Their leader, a shadowy figure known only as the Shadow, had a well-deserved reputation for being a brilliant tactician and a stalwart supporter of fairness and equity in the world.

Sarah was led through a web of danger and deception as she descended into the underbelly of the organization. She saw the seedier side of humanity, including the desperation that drove some people to commit unspeakable acts, the trafficking of illegal goods, and the fight for survival in a lawless domain. But even in the midst of the mayhem, there were glimpses of compassion and camaraderie. These moments served as reminders that the human spirit is resilient, even in the darkest of times.

When Sarah was getting closer to the center of the underbelly, she ran into a face-to-face confrontation with the Shadow. The enigmatic leader, who was obscured by the shadows, gave off an air of unshakeable authority and tenacity. The Shadow spoke in a low, commanding whisper that was laced with a mix of trepidation and resolve.

The Shadow was appreciative of Sarah's bravery and the commitment she had shown to the cause. They discussed the regime's iron grip on society, as well as the injustices and suffering that were inflicted upon those who were oppressed. They explained that the underbelly held the key to destabilizing the power structure of the regime. The underbelly offered a network of resources, information, and allies that had the potential to tip the scales in favor of the resistance.

They banded together to form an alliance, which was a collaboration between the unyielding determination of the resistance and the expertise of the Black Hand regarding the intricacies of the underbelly's operations. It was crystal clear what Sarah's mission was: to gather vital intelligence, expose corruption, and strike at the core of the regime's control.

Sarah came across a diverse cast of characters when she was working her way through the underbelly of the city. These included thieves with good intentions, informants with hidden agendas, and revolutionaries who had given up everything for the cause. They discussed the atrocities committed by the regime as well as the lives that were shattered as a result of its tyranny. Sarah's resolve was strengthened by each new experience, which fueled her resoluteness to bring about transformation.

As the hours turned into days, Sarah and the Black Hand began to work toward their goal of dismantling the regime's core principles. They caused supply lines to be disrupted, they disclosed sensitive information, and they planted the seeds of doubt within the ranks of the regime. The underbelly evolved into a battleground for covert operations, creating a dynamic dance between darkness and light at all times.

On the other hand, the further they dove into the underbelly of the situation, the greater the risks became. As the regime became more aware of the growing danger, it increased its efforts to locate the members of the resistance. There was a constant risk of betrayal because there were informants and double agents working against them to sabotage their progress.

Sarah was put in perilous situations at every turn, and her gut instincts and her ability to trust were put to the test. But she did not show any sign of wavering. The seedy underbelly had become her second home, and it was there that she had the opportunity to observe the resiliency of the human spirit. As a result, she was prepared to fight tooth and nail to defend the fragile threads of hope that held them all together.

Sarah was well aware of the fact that her transformation had taken place as she was getting ready to emerge from the depths of the underbelly. She had gotten a glimpse of the darkest corners of their world, confronted the abyss head-on, and emerged from those experiences stronger. The seedy underbelly had developed into a source of resiliency and unity, serving as a demonstration of the unyielding spirit of those who had the audacity to resist.

Sarah ascended to the surface armed with the information she had gained and the alliances she had forged in the underbelly. She was prepared to carry on the fight against the oppressive rule of the regime. The descent had been perilous, but it had also exposed a wellspring of strength and determination within her; this was a force that would carry her forward no matter the cost.

Chapter 7: Broken Bonds: Betrayal in the Wasteland

S arah Thompson was confronted by a desolate landscape that spread out before her like a barren expanse of despair. It was a jarring reminder of the toll that their struggle against the repressive regime had taken. As she progressed further into the barren landscape, she was unable to shake the gnawing sense of unease that she had been experiencing ever since she had entered it.

Sarah had left the relative safety of the resistance hideout in order to follow a lead that held the potential to provide useful information that would assist in their cause. However, the wasteland was a perilous place, replete with peril and apprehension around every corner. Underneath the surface of this land lay severed connections and shattered trust between people.

Sarah continued to move forward while keeping her senses on high alert and her eyes peeled for any signs of life on the horizon. A sense of desolation pervaded the environment, which was characterized by broken down ruins, twisted metal, and a pervasive lack of human habitation. The wasteland bore the scars of the regime's cruelty, a glaring reminder of the results of their actions on the environment.

As Sarah continued to move deeper into the wasteland, the weight of isolation began to become apparent in her footsteps. A feeling of vulnerability that she had never felt before crept over her as a result of the absence of her fellow rebels as well as the persistent danger of betrayal. Her trust had been shattered by the harsh realities of their world, so every noise and every movement sent her nerves into overdrive.

Sarah noticed a figure off in the distance; it was a solitary traveler with wary eyes. They moved guardedly closer to one another, approaching each other with caution. The wanderer introduced himself as Caleb, claiming to be a person who had managed to escape the regime's brutal rule. He asserted that he possessed vital information that could swing the balance of power in their favor.

Sarah listened attentively as Caleb recounted his story, which was about overcoming obstacles while enduring loss and suffering. Despite her lingering misgivings, Sarah paid close attention as Caleb spoke. He talked about a clandestine network of dissidents, people who were once trusted allies but had turned to the regime and betrayed their comrades for the sake of personal gain. These traitors had infiltrated the resistance on a deep level, posing as allies while secretly providing vital information to the resistance's adversaries.

The news came as a devastating blow to Sarah, shattering the fragile trust that she had placed in the other members of the resistance. Their resistance was in danger of collapsing as a result of the broken bonds of betrayal, which cast doubt on the very foundation of their fight for justice. Nevertheless, Sarah was able to see through the chaos and recognize the importance of confronting this truth head-on.

Sarah, armed with her newly acquired awareness of the need to exercise extreme caution, dove headfirst into the task of identifying the betrayers hiding among their ranks. She investigated every interaction, carefully analyzed each member of the resistance, and tracked down the breadcrumb trail of questionable occurrences. Her natural instincts were honed by the possibility of betrayal, and the wasteland became her hunting ground as a result.

Sarah's tireless efforts to expose the betrayers continued through the day and into the night. Her heart became burdened with disillusionment and rage as the weight of each revelation gradually settled upon her shoulders. She found individuals whose loyalty remained unwavering and who stood resolute in the face of adversity. However, for every broken bond that she uncovered, she also found steadfast allies.

As the truth became more apparent, Sarah was forced to confront the spies one by one. Each confrontation was marked by tense exchanges and the dissolution of friendships. The grip of the regime had manipulated and twisted the minds of those who she had once trusted, but their betrayal only served to fuel her determination to bring those responsible for her oppression to justice.

Caleb emerged as a rock of stability amidst all of this upheaval, despite the fact that his own history was marred by the anguish of betrayal. Together, they devised a plan, which involved compiling evidence and rallying supporters who were still committed to the cause. The wasteland turned into a training ground, a place where new bonds were created and trust was reconstructed from the ruins of previously broken faith.

After the traitors were found out, Sarah and her remaining allies regrouped, their resolve having been strengthened by the ordeal of being betrayed that they had gone through. The wasteland had exposed the most depraved aspects of human nature, but it had also demonstrated the resiliency of their spirit. It served as a reminder that even in the face of betrayal, they continued to fight for justice and freedom.

Sarah was getting ready to leave the wasteland behind, and she took the scars of broken bonds with her. These scars served as a constant reminder of how fragile trust can be in a world that has been ravaged by tyranny. However, she also brought with her a revitalized sense of purpose, which was strengthened by the realization that their fight was not only against the regime, but also against the corrosive forces that threatened to tear them apart from the inside.

Chapter 8: The Lost Innocence: Children of a Darkened Era

When Sarah Thompson saw the plight of the children who were caught in the grip of the repressive regime, she felt the weight of a darkened era settle heavily upon her shoulders. This was a moment that she will never forget. Their naiveté had been taken from them, and in its place had been implanted a jaded resiliency that was the product of the challenging experiences they had gone through. They were the helpless victims of this cruel world, forced to become adults at an earlier age than they should have.

Sarah went on an adventure deep within a forsaken orphanage, the walls of which were stained with the remains of a hope that had been lost. The stench of desolation hung heavy in the air, and the echoes of children's laughter were replaced by a solemn silence. The irreparable harm done to an entire generation is brought home in a way that will break your heart when you see the innocence that has been taken from these children.

Sarah's heart broke as she made her way through the crumbling hallways and caught glimpses of people with sunken eyes and weathered features. The children, who had previously been filled with delight and awe, now bore burdens that no child should have to bear. They had been exposed to things like starvation, fear, and loss at a young age, their childhood being robbed from them by a world that was consumed by darkness.

In the midst of their hopeless situation, Sarah made an effort to shed some light on the situation. She arranged for them to have impromptu classes, where she taught them how to read and write while also fostering their natural curiosity and desire to learn. She encouraged them to express themselves and seek solace in their own creative endeavors as a means of reclaiming some of the innocence that had been taken from them through the use of art and storytelling.

But Sarah was also aware that the children required other things in addition to their education. They required someone to provide them with emotional support, consistency, and a sense of belonging. She encouraged the children to support one another and find strength in their common experiences by organizing group activities and cultivating a sense of community.

The children, who were traumatized but incredibly resilient, gradually built up their trust in Sarah and the other caring individuals who offered a helping hand. Their eyes, which had previously been lifeless and dull, started to show signs of regaining some hope. Sarah was able to catch glimpses of their innate resilience, as well as their ability to adapt and live through even the most trying conditions.

Sarah came to realize that the children were not merely helpless victims; rather, they were resolute warriors in their own right as their relationship with her and the children deepened. They were possessed of a spirit that defied being stifled and an unyielding determination to prevail despite the obstacles that stood in their way. Sarah was able to unearth previously unknown abilities, dreams, and goals by listening to the stories of others who had persevered in spite of the darkness that pervaded their world.

However, the regime's control extended all the way into the children's home. Sarah was a witness to the regime's efforts to indoctrinate the children by rewriting their history, manipulating the children's impressionable minds with propaganda, and otherwise attempting to rewrite their past. It became abundantly clear that the struggle to protect the children's innocence was not confined to the confines of the orphanage; rather, it permeated the very essence of the mission that the resistance was attempting to accomplish.

Sarah and her allies came up with a strategy in order to shield the children from any further attempts at manipulation. They created covert classrooms in the orphanage's most inconspicuous nooks and crannies so that the truth could be guarded, the children could learn about their own history, and the seeds of critical thinking and independent thought could be sown.

As a defiant act of resistance against the regime's attempts to erase their humanity, they collaborated on the creation of stories and artworks that captured the essence of the innocence that had been taken from them. The works of art that were produced by the children became a representation of optimism, a testomony to the tenacity of the human spirit, and a reminder that even in the most difficult of circumstances, the flame of innocence can be rekindled.

When Sarah left the orphanage, she took with her the burden of the children's experiences as well as the responsibility to safeguard their future. Her regret over the loss of their childhood innocence served as the impetus for her resolve to free them from the control the regime exercised over their world. She vowed that she would fight not only for their freedom but also for the opportunity to regain their lost childhoods, which she saw as a ray of light in the midst of the darkness that threatened to consume them all.

Chapter 9: A Ray of Light: Hope Amidst Desolation

Sarah Thompson and the other weary souls who had fought against the oppressive regime were beginning to lose hope when, out of the utter desolation, a ray of light broke through the suffocating darkness and offered a glimmer of hope to all of them. It was a guiding light that invigorated their spirits and reignited their resolve to reclaim their world.

The ravages of the city's decline were etched into the landscape, and Sarah found herself standing on a rooftop with a view of the city below. The propaganda of the regime was still a significant factor; however, there was a freshfound sense of cohesion and purpose coursing through the veins of the resistance. They had endured a plethora of tests, seen the darkest depths of humanity's capacity for cruelty, and emerged from those experiences more resilient.

As Sarah surveyed the landscape of the city, she noticed pockets of resistance growing like defiant wildflowers in the midst of the destruction. Those who had previously been unable to speak out were gaining the confidence to do so and speaking out against the dictatorship of the regime. As citizens, who had previously accepted their destinies, started to pull themselves up from the ashes, the air crackled with the sound of change.

Sarah and the other members of the resistance planned and carried out acts of civil disobedience, which hampered the functioning of the regime's apparatus and questioned its authority. They organized secret gatherings to discuss strategies and information and painted messages of hope on the crumbling walls. The voice of the resistance as a whole had grown to the point where it could no longer be ignored as it called for freedom and justice.

Their message spread like wildfire, kindling a spark of rebellion in the hearts of those who had been subjugated for a very long time. As more and more citizens began to question the regime's dishonest narratives, the propaganda of the regime began to fail. They longed for a brighter tomorrow, a second chance to reconstruct their shattered world on the principles of compassion and equality.

Sarah was present during the beginning of grass-roots movements, which consisted of citizens banding together to reclaim their neighborhoods, rebuild infrastructure, and offer assistance to those who were in need. The efforts of the resistance had set off a chain reaction, a domino effect of defiance that reverberated all over the city.

In a desperate attempt to stem the rising tide of discontent, the regime's response was to step up its already aggressive tactics. The resistance was put through increasingly difficult circumstances, including an increase in the number of violent confrontations and crackdowns. But they did not yield, their spirits remaining unyielding, and they refused to be quieted.

Sarah noticed that people from a diverse range of backgrounds were joining the resistance as it gained momentum. People in positions of authority such as teachers, artists, and doctors, as well as former regime supporters, came to the realization that the regime was deeply corrupt and made the decision to take a stance in favor of justice. As different skills and points of view came together to form a formidable force, the resistance's greatest strength turned out to be the diversity that existed within its ranks.

Sarah witnessed acts of extraordinary bravery and compassion while she was in the middle of the chaos. Strangers reached out to those in need and offered assistance, even as they put their own lives in jeopardy to shield the helpless. The unbreakable bonds that were forged in the fire of their struggle are a testament to the strength that can be achieved through unity and solidarity.

The glimmer of hope grew stronger and shed more light on the way forward with each successive insignificant victory. Sarah was aware that the conflict was not yet over and that the path that lay ahead would be fraught with difficulties and demands for sacrifice. However, she was also aware that so long as there was even a sliver of optimism, their struggle would not be in vain.

The glimmer of hope that emanated from their collective fortitude spread like wildfire, motivating the cities and communities in the surrounding area to rise up against the oppressors in their own lives. The initial glimmer of discontent had grown into a raging inferno, which threatened to consume the authoritarian regime's hold on power.

As Sarah took in the altered scenery, her chest expanded with a sense that was equal parts pride and humility. The city was no longer a desolate wasteland; rather, it stood as a testament to the indomitable will of the human spirit to reconstruct and reimagine a future free from tyranny.

They were able to emerge from the depths of darkness thanks to the solitary beam of light that had transformed into a beacon for them. They were reminded that even in the darkest of times, there is always a chance for something better. The idea that a better world was within their reach kept the resistance moving forward, and it was the driving force behind their success.

While Sarah was getting ready to take her place on the front lines of the revolution, she was carrying the burden of everyone's hopes and dreams on her shoulders. The glimmer of hope had become a blazing beacon of resistance, piercing the cloud of despondency and illuminating the way to a better future — a future in which justice, freedom, and humanity would prevail over the forces that oppressed them.

Chapter 10: Whispers of Rebellion: Seeds of Change

Within the murky depths of uncertainty, rumblings of disobedience reverberated through the air, transporting the germinating seeds of change to every crevice of their fragmented world. Sarah Thompson was in the midst of a defining moment, a reckoning that would put the tenacity of the resistance to the test and decide the future of their dystopian society.

The regime, sensing the growing strength of the tremors of dissent, responded with an increase in aggressive behavior. It increased the amount of surveillance it carried out and resorted to harsh methods in order to stifle any hint of resistance or rebellion. But Sarah was aware that the time for remaining silent had long since passed, and that the moment had come to speak out against the repressive regime.

She gathered what was left of the resistance and addressed her comrades in a determined tone as she addressed them. The resistance of the group as a whole, combined with their unyielding faith in a more favorable future, had planted the seeds of transformation. The time had come to reap the benefits of their labor and go toe-to-toe with the regime.

The resistance had laboriously planned their strategy over the course of several months, paying close attention to the vulnerabilities of the regime, working covertly within its ranks, and gathering crucial intel. They were well aware that the key to their success lay in their capacity to launch an attack against the weakest points of the regime.

The information about the impending uprising began to spread through their network in the form of rumors, reaching every dissident, dissident, and oppressed soul who yearned for liberation. The resistance had evolved into a powerful source of motivation, serving as a rallying cry for anyone who had the audacity to imagine a world in which tyranny did not exist.

As the day of reckoning drew near, there was an increase in anticipation along with a surge of nervous energy that ran through the resistance. Sarah took her place at the front of the line, the fear and resolve in her heart beating at the same rapid pace. The time for waiting was over; in their decisive confrontation with the regime, they would either prevail or fail.

The streets turned into a battleground, which descended into a cacophonous symphony of both resistance and oppression. The regime's control was undermined as a result of the guerrilla tactics employed by the resistance, which rendered their surveillance networks ineffective. Sarah navigated the urban labyrinth with the help of her comrades, striking strategic targets and freeing communities that had been oppressed.

The regime's response was one of brutal force, with its enforcers being let loose in a last-ditch effort to preserve the regime's hold on power. The battles were bloody, many people were killed, and the scars of the conflict are still visible on the landscape of the city. However, the resistance kept moving forward, driven by a common goal to create a world free from fear and oppression for all people.

The rumors of a rebellion became more audible after each victory, which encouraged even the most hesitant individuals to support the cause. The citizens' defiance was fueled by the bravery of the resistance, and they flooded out onto the streets in large numbers. They fought with tenacity, knowing that a change was already beginning to take root within their hearts.

As the uprising gained steam, the seemingly impregnable shield that the regime used to protect itself began to crack. As the regime's web of lies was exposed by the truth, propaganda began to lose its power. The once obedient enforcers began to question their allegiance and discovered a sense of community in the unyielding pursuit of justice by the resistance.

When Sarah turned around, she found herself face to face with the regime's most ruthless enforcer — a personification of the cruel nature of the repressive regime. The climactic confrontation was a clash of ideologies as well as personal grudges, and it was intense to say the least. It was a battle not just of physical strength, but of the unconquerable spirit that refused to bow down to tyranny. This was a battle.

In the thick of the battle, Sarah's tenacity and tactical acumen came in handy and made her an unstoppable force. She outmanoeuvred her adversary, which led to the regime's deepest secrets being revealed to the outside world. The vanquishing of the enforcer came to represent the success of the resistance and marked a turning point in the struggle for freedom.

Sarah stood before a crowd that consisted of citizens as well as rebels as the regime collapsed under the weight of its own corruption. Her voice, which had previously been barely audible, now resounded with an unwavering determination. She acknowledged the hardships that were endured, the lives that were lost, and the sacrifices that were made. But she also spoke of the beginnings of a rebellion, one that was already well on its way to becoming a full-fledged uprising and one that would reshape the world they lived in.

Sarah and the other rebels she was fighting alongside began the laborious process of rebuilding after the remnants of the regime were thrown into chaos. They established a new order, one that was founded on justice, compassion, and equality in all relationships. They mended the frayed ties that held society together, cultivating a sense of unity and a shared purpose that would stop the atrocities of the past from being repeated.

In the aftermath of their victory, whispers of rebellion transformed into songs of triumph; these songs served as a reminder that even in the most difficult of times, the power to change the world lay within the hands of those who were oppressed.

Sarah was awestruck by the profound change that had taken place as she contemplated the ruins of the previous government while she stood there. The germination of the seeds of change had resulted in the destruction of the concrete that represented oppression and the blossoming of a new era of hope. It was a demonstration of the strength that can be achieved through perseverance, unity, and the unyielding spirit of those who refuse to accept the status quo.

And as the echoes of their struggle began to fade into the annals of history, the whispers of rebellion continued to ripple through time, serving as a constant reminder of the unstoppable power of the human spirit to shape its own destiny.

Chapter 11: The Power Struggle: Kings and Pawns

The fall of the regime was followed by the beginning of a new power struggle, which manifested itself as a delicate dance between those who were vying for control in the aftermath of their hard-fought victory. As the beginnings of a new order began to take root, Sarah Thompson found herself caught in the middle of a convoluted web of shifting allegiances, shifting alliances, and shifting rivalries.

As the dust began to settle, various factions within the resistance competed with one another for influence. Each of these factions had their own unique perspective on what the future held. Others, wary of the potential risks associated with social upheaval, advocated for a more measured approach, while others advocated for a radical reorganization of society. Sarah found herself in the middle of a power struggle, and her opinion was given significant consideration during the deliberation process.

People who saw an opportunity to make money for themselves by taking advantage of the power vacuum were at the center of the conflict. They skulked in the shadows, pulling strings and orchestrating events in a way that suited their own goals and aspirations. Sarah's sharp intuition made it possible for her to see through their lies, and she made up her mind to defend the precarious harmony that they had finally accomplished.

She called meetings and encouraged everyone involved to find some area of agreement and work together toward a unified goal. Compromises were reached, alliances were established, and a concerted effort to create a society that is just and equitable began to take shape as a result of these efforts. The struggle for power shifted from being an internal battle to an external battle, a battle against the remnants of the old regime who sought to regain control. This battle was against the remnants of the old regime.

Sarah and her allies were aware of the need to strike a delicate balance in order to achieve their goals, which included both the responsible use of power and the prevention of the establishment of a new authoritarian regime. They put in place a system of checks and balances to make sure that no single person or group could amass an excessive amount of authority or influence.

However, as the struggle for power intensified, Sarah realized that even within the resistance, there were some individuals who were willing to betray their comrades in order to advance their own personal agendas. As individuals sought to advance their own agendas at the expense of the collective, it led to the emergence of kings and pawns in the system. Sarah was well aware of the delicate nature of trust and how easy it was for it to be betrayed and how challenging it was to regain.

She proceeded with extreme circumspection and good judgment as she navigated the perilous waters of the power struggle. She distanced herself from people whose primary motivation was to advance their own self-interest while simultaneously forming alliances with people whose honesty and dedication to the cause were unshakeable. It was a tricky dance trying to strike a balance between the competing priorities of maintaining unity while also remaining vigilant.

Both Sarah's leadership and her moral compass became guiding beacons that encouraged others to maintain their unwavering commitment to working toward a more equitable society. She exposed those who sought to manipulate the power struggle for their own personal gain by utilizing her strategic acumen, thereby protecting the resistance's honor and keeping it intact.

In the midst of the struggle for power, Sarah came to the realization that it was essential to give more agency to the people. She worked to ensure that the voices of those who were marginalized and oppressed were heard while advocating for more openness and inclusivity in society. Movements at the grassroots level and community organizing came to play an important role in the mission of the resistance, laying a firm groundwork for the new order that its members aspired to establish.

Sarah steadfastly refused to be swayed by the allure of authority as the struggle for power continued to rage. She did not waver in her commitment to the principles that had served as the impetus for the resistance ever since it was first organized. These principles included a dedication to justice and equality as well as the conviction that power should be exercised with responsibility and compassion.

Sarah's unyielding determination and keen sense of justice contributed to the resolution of the power struggle, which she helped to steer in that direction. The resistance succeeded in becoming more powerful and united, and it is now prepared to face the challenges that lie ahead. They understood that true power did not come from dominance, but rather from the capacity to elevate and give agency to the voices of those who were oppressed.

In the end, a system of governance was developed that struck a delicate balance. It allowed for the freedoms of the individual, safeguarded the rights of all citizens, and made certain that no single person or group could exercise unchecked power. The struggle for power had given way to a collective responsibility, an understanding that the new world they were building required constant vigilance and a commitment to the principles for which they had fought. This understanding had taken the place of the power struggle.

As Sarah surveyed the new terrain of their society, she was aware that the struggle for power would leave an indelible mark on their record for all time. It served as a reminder of the dangers of unchecked authority as well as the necessity of remaining vigilant against the forces that sought to undermine the freedom that they had worked so hard to achieve.

Chapter 12: Unholy Alliances: Survival at Any Cost

In the wake of the battle for power, a chilling realization dawned on Sarah Thompson and the surviving members of the resistance. As the new order started to take shape, unholy alliances began to form. These were alliances that were formed for the purpose of serving one's own self-interest in the quest to survive at any cost. Sarah found herself in the precarious position of navigating a perilous landscape, one in which trust was in short supply and betrayal lurked around every corner.

Individuals who had once fought side by side against a common foe had become corrupted by the allure of power and influence. They had built a fragile unity, but there were factions among them, and greed and personal ambition threatened to tear it apart. The shadows of their dystopian world began to seep into the cracks of their new society, eroding the basis upon which they had fought so hard to build justice and equality.

Sarah was aware that their ability to unearth the truth and expose those who had compromised their principles in order to advance their own interests was essential to the maintenance of the freedom that they had fought so valiantly to win. She made a solemn oath to defend the new order from the corrosive forces of corruption and to serve as a sentinel against the creeping gloom.

In her quest for justice, Sarah went to the seedy parts of the new society, where shady dealings and covert operations flourished, in order to investigate these places. She came into contact with people who had prospered under the previous government and who had viewed the anarchy as an opportunity to amass wealth and power. They had completely abandoned any semblance of decency, forming alliances with less than savory characters in order to take advantage of the loopholes in the new system.

When Sarah saw the values they had fought for being eroded, her heart sank. These were the very values that had inspired their rebellion, and yet here they were being eroded. The instinct to survive had taken precedence over principles, and the unholy alliances that had formed posed a threat to suffocate the hopes and dreams that they had held so dearly in such high regard.

Sarah's determination did not waver as she searched for any remaining voices of dissent. She rallied those who continued to believe in the principles of justice and equality, as well as those who refused to compromise their principles in exchange for personal gain. Together, they skulked around in the shadows as they dug up the murky details that were threatening to bring their fragile society to its knees.

Sarah and her allies confronted those individuals who had deviated from the path of righteousness as the unholy alliances became increasingly brazen. They brought the wrongdoers to justice and reclaimed the principles for which they had fought by exposing the double dealing and corruption that had permeated their ranks.

However, the road to redemption was littered with perils at every turn. Those who had experienced power were hesitant to give up their hold on it once they had it because the alliances that had formed were difficult to dismantle. The opposition that Sarah and her allies faced was fierce, and it came from both inside and outside of their ranks.

An atmosphere of mistrust and paranoia had developed as a result of the mentality of "survival at any cost." It had become a luxury that only a select few could afford, and the possibility of being betrayed lurked in the background of every interaction. Sarah was aware that in order to reclaim the vision that they had fought for, they would need to confront the darkness head-on, exposing it to the light of truth and unwavering determination in order to reclaim the vision that they had fought for.

In order to prevail in the war against the unholy alliances, it was necessary to make sacrifices and maintain a firm resolve. Allegiances were put to the test as friends were betrayed and turned into enemies. Sarah was a witness to the lives that were lost, the friendships that were shattered, and the ideals that they held dear that were tainted by the stain of betrayal as a result of their struggle.

But despite the challenges, there was still a glimmer of hope that remained. The voices of those who opposed the current order grew louder, buoyed by the unyielding spirit of those individuals who refused to give in to the temptation of power. Sarah and her allies were successful in forging new alliances, ones that were founded on a common set of values and an unwavering dedication to serving the greater good.

They banded together and started a movement to free their society from the grip of the unholy alliances, which were holding it hostage. They rallied those who had lost hope, those who had lost their magic, and those who were on the margins of society, uniting them under the banner of justice and equality. The dissemination of the truth turned into a weapon, as it exposed the dishonest alliances and inspired a movement of resistance.

In the fight against the unholy alliances, we experienced both success and failure, and we made sacrifices along the way. It required steadfast bravery and a determination that could not be shaken. On the other hand, Sarah and her allies stubbornly refused to give in to the darkness. They were driven by the conviction that their society could be redeemed, and that it was possible for the seeds of justice and equality to once again germinate and grow.

As the new dawn broke, the unholy alliances quickly disintegrated under the pressure of the truth and the wrath of the righteous. The survivors emerged from the wreckage of the destruction, scarred but resolute in their determination to reconstruct their society. They were able to avoid repeating the errors of the past by developing a system that provided protection against the insidious allure of power as well as the corrupting influences of greed.

In the end, Sarah found herself on the edge of a society that had been irrevocably altered, a society that bore the marks of the unholy alliances that had threatened to consume it. The mentality of "survival at any cost" had been defeated, and in its place was a collective determination to uphold the values for which they had fought. They had gained the insight through their struggle that the cost of survival must never compromise the integrity of their ideals, no matter how dire the situation may become.

Chapter 13: Shattered Dreams: A World in Chaos

In the aftermath of the power struggle and the revealing of unholy alliances, Sarah Thompson and the remnants of the resistance were confronted with a harsh reality. They were shown a world in chaos, where shattered dreams and broken promises cast a long shadow over their once hopeful vision.

The fierce conflicts they had fought and the sacrifices they had made seemed insignificant in comparison to the enormous difficulties that lay in wait for them in the future. Following the collapse of the regime, there was a void in power that was quickly filled by a wave of anarchy and instability. The fragile social fabric was ripped to shreds as factions competed with one another for control of the new world and sought to fashion it in their own image.

Sarah couldn't help but feel a profound sense of loss as she surveyed the devastated landscape as she looked around her. It appeared as though the hopes for justice, equality, and a better future were a long way off; they were merely relics of an idealistic era. The power struggle and the unholy alliances had left deep scars, which were etched into the very core of their world. These scars ran deep.

The cohesion and common goal that had driven their uprising in the past were no longer present. When it was removed, discord and division took its place. The betrayal and pursuit of one's own interests had planted the seeds of mistrust, which eventually took root and tore apart the bonds of solidarity and camaraderie. The dashed expectations were a heavy burden on their community's conscience, and they posed a danger of falling into an abyss of hopelessness as a result.

Sarah was aware that the world they had envisioned could not be reconstructed overnight, and that in order to do so, it would take resiliency, determination, and an unwavering faith in the inherent goodness of humanity. She rounded up those individuals who had not wavered in their dedication to the cause, and she rallied them to take on the mayhem head-on.

Together, they worked toward the common goal of reestablishing some semblance of order amidst the anarchy, of rescuing the shattered dreams, and of reassembling a society that would be able to emerge from the ruins. Sarah exerted a lot of effort in order to patch up the damaged relationships and close the rifts that existed in their shattered world. She listened to the complaints and fears of those who were disillusioned, offering comfort and direction in the face of ambiguity.

They initiated programs to offer assistance, support, and stability to those who were most in need because these individuals had been the ones to bear the brunt of the unrest. During the most difficult of times, they erected makeshift shelters, dispersed food and supplies, and offered a supportive shoulder for people to lean on. It was an effort to keep a glimmer of hope alive amidst the disarray, to demonstrate to those whose world had been shattered that humanity and compassion were not entirely extinguished.

However, it seemed impossible to overcome the obstacles. The divisions that already existed within society became even more pronounced, and the struggle for power became much more intense. The power struggle and the unholy alliances continued to reverberate, which cast a long shadow of uncertainty over their collective future. The dreams that they had once held dear appeared to be nothing more than a far-off illusion now.

At each and every turn, Sarah and her allies were met with opposition. Their efforts to rebuild and heal were met with skepticism and resistance from those who had lost faith in the possibility of a better world. Those who had lost faith in the possibility of a better world. Scars that ran deep had been left behind as a result of the chaos, scars that threatened to consume what was left of the hope that had been preserved.

Nevertheless, there were flashes of resiliency and determination even in the midst of the chaos. As people began to rediscover their humanity, we saw a rise in the number of seemingly insignificant acts of kindness and compassion. Sarah and her allies took care of these sparks and fanned them into flames of change because they were aware that even in the darkest of times, a single ember could ignite a revolution. They did this because they knew that even in the darkest of times, a single ember could ignite a revolution.

Piece by laborious piece, the shattered dreams started to piece themselves back together again. The unwavering dedication that Sarah and her allies displayed, as well as their refusal to give in to the chaos that was threatening to engulf them, served as an inspiration to those around them. They banded together, realizing that their power lay in their cohesiveness, and fought the battle against despondency as a united front.

They continued to put forth the effort, and as the days turned into weeks, and the weeks into months, they started to see some results. As individuals put aside their disagreements and collaborated toward a common goal of restoring order to their shattered world, the shattered society started to slowly heal and begin to function again. In the face of adversity, the scars from their past became symbols of their resiliency, and their dreams, despite being changed in some ways, became even more powerful.

Sarah took in the sight of the world that she had fought so hard to save, a world that was still marred by chaos but now possessed of a revitalized sense of purpose. The shattered hopes had given way to a newly discovered resolve — a resolve to rise from the ashes and rebuild, to gain wisdom from the errors of the past, and to forge a future that held the promise of a better tomorrow. Those dreams had been shattered, but they had given way to a newfound determination.

Despite everything that was going wrong, people continued to have hope. The broken dreams, despite being excruciating reminders of the hardships they had endured in the past, laid the groundwork for a fresh start. Sarah and her allies would proceed to navigate the uncertainties and weather the storms that threatened to extinguish the flames of progress despite the fact that they were facing an uphill battle.

Because even in a world torn apart by anarchy, there was still a glimmer of optimism, a glimmer of possibility that hinted at a future in which shattered dreams could be reassembled and a world that had been consumed by darkness could be reborn into the light.

Chapter 14: The Masked Truth: Deception Unveiled

Sarah Thompson and the remnants of the resistance found out in the aftermath of the chaos and the efforts to rebuild that their shattered world still held secrets, secrets that were carefully concealed behind a web of deception. As they peeled back the layers of their society, the hidden truth became apparent, exposing a shadowy underside that posed a risk to their laboriously achieved advancement.

Even though Sarah had always been watchful, the events that transpired left her in a state of disbelief. She uncovered a shadowy network that was operating in the background, and she discovered that there was a puppet master pulling strings and manipulating events for their own benefit. The very foundation of their new society was built on deceit and incomplete information, which cast suspicion on the intentions of those who had previously presented themselves as allies.

As Sarah continued to delve deeper into the murky depths of the masked truth, she came to the realization that the lies ran much deeper than she could have ever imagined they would. Institutions that were supposed to protect and serve the people had been compromised, and those in power were using them as tools to maintain their control over the population. The levels of dishonesty reached all the way up to the most powerful members of their society.

Sarah and her allies diligently searched for evidence and pieced together clues that revealed the scope of the deception. By following the trail of breadcrumbs that led to the puppet master behind the scenes, they were able to decipher the complex web of lies that had been woven. Each new piece of information brought them one step closer to uncovering the true nature of the conspiracy, but it also put their determination and their capacity for trust to the test.

As individuals who were once considered comrades but were later revealed to be collaborators in the grand deception, the betrayals left a deep wound. Sarah was well aware that giving in to hopelessness was not an option, despite the fact that the weight of the masked truth posed a threat to crush their spirit. They had fought too hard and made too many sacrifices to allow the puppet master's manipulations to continue without any resistance.

They came up with a strategy to expose the truth and break the puppet master's control over their society by working together and creating a plan. They depended on their surviving allies, those whose unflinching loyalty had allowed them to prevail despite the difficulties they had faced. They made an effort to rally those who had become disillusioned with their leaders by reaching out to those individuals in an effort to convince them to support their cause.

As more people joined the resistance movement, the puppet master's hold on power started to loosen. The concealed reality became visible, which compelled those who had been complicit in the deception to face the consequences of their actions. Sarah and her allies fought a battle on multiple fronts, one of which was against the puppet master and their minions, as well as the apathy and skepticism that had taken hold of the masses of people who had lost faith in the government.

The fight to uncover the concealed reality exacted a significant toll on everyone involved. There were human lives that were lost, sacrifices that were made, and trust that could not be restored. But despite everything that happened, Sarah never wavered in her resolve; her determination was unwavering. She was aware that the path to justice was not an easy one, and that it was littered with challenges and roadblocks at every turn of the journey.

Sarah looked into the eyes of their adversary, which was a personification of the deception that had plagued their society, during their final confrontation with the puppet master. The conflict was not just a test of one's physical prowess, but also of one's wits and the efficacy of the truth. It was a fight to free their society from the grip of deception and manipulation, which had held it captive for so long.

Sarah exposed the crimes committed by the puppet master, bringing to light the extent of their deceit, using every fiber of her being to do so. The hidden truth came to the surface, shedding a harsh light on the manipulations carried out by the puppet master. The time had come to take stock of everything.

The hidden truth came to light as the empire of the puppet master fell apart, which resulted in the creation of a vacuum in its wake. The shattered lives, the broken trust, and the scars of deception etched deep into their souls were all things that Sarah and her allies considered when they took stock of the damage. But in addition to that, they saw glimmers of hope, which were the seeds of truth that had been planted in the fertile ground of a society that demanded transparency and accountability.

Their shattered world, which was once again confronted with the consequences of deception, stood at a fork in the road. They had realized the significance of remaining vigilant, the need to call into question the narratives that were being presented to them, and the significance of maintaining unity in the face of dishonesty. The road to a society that is just and equitable was not without its obstacles, but those individuals were resolute in their goal to rebuild on the principles of honesty and integrity as their basis.

As Sarah took in the surroundings, she felt a sense of victory that was simultaneously bitter and sweet. The long-concealed reality had finally been exposed, leaving wounds that would never completely heal.

However, in its wake, a newly discovered resolve emerged: a commitment to never allow deception to take hold again, and to forge a society in which the truth would be the guiding light.

Chapter 15: In the Clutches of Fear: Paranoia Takes Hold

While the rest of the broken world was trying to pick up the pieces and move on from the aftermath of the deception, Sarah Thompson and the few people who were left in the resistance found themselves caught in a different kind of darkness. The feeling of paranoia started to spread throughout their society like a poisonous vine, and it eventually made its way into people's hearts and minds.

The uncovering of the concealed reality had left deep scars, jolting the people's sense of trust in their leaders and planting the seeds of uncertainty in their minds. Fear transformed into a covert, all-pervasive force that lingered in the shadows, muttering uncertainties and suspicions into the ears of those who were already worn out. There was a blurring of the lines between friends and foes as individuals began to question the intentions of even those who were closest to them.

Sarah understood the stealthy nature of this new danger, which was one that could destroy everything they had worked so hard to achieve. She was a witness to the breakdown of the group's unity and the deterioration of the sense of community that they had labored so diligently to construct. In their interactions with one another, paranoia crept in and bred distrust and isolation, ultimately severing the frail bonds that had just started to mend.

She was adamant about confronting the growing paranoia head-on, and so she rallied the remaining allies. They arranged get-togethers for the community, with the goals of promoting open conversation and fostering empathy. They endeavored to establish forums in which individuals could express their worries and anxieties and collaborate with one another to identify areas of agreement.

However, the fear had already taken hold, and their attempts to eradicate it were unsuccessful. Individuals were left vulnerable and susceptible to the corrosive effects of paranoia as a result of the deep scars that were left behind by deception. There was a proliferation of rumors and whispers, which added more fuel to the flames of mistrust. They had fought so hard to rebuild society, but now it seemed like it was on the verge of destroying itself.

Sarah was aware that in order to free themselves from the grips of fear, they needed to address the factors that contributed to it. They initiated educational campaigns and spread information in an effort to debunk the falsehoods and propaganda that contributed to the spread of paranoia. They brought attention to the significance of critical thinking and encouraged people to question and analyze the information that they took in by asking them to highlight the importance of critical thinking.

However, it turned out to be a difficult fight to overcome our anxiety. It required more than just logic and reason; rather, it demanded a collective effort to overcome ingrained insecurities and traumas that had been carried for a very long time. Sarah and her allies worked tirelessly to provide support and counseling because they realized that mending the wounds caused by deception was essential to releasing themselves from the hold that paranoia had on them.

In spite of the difficulty, there were a few rays of hope that shone through. People who had allowed themselves to be overcome by paranoia started to discover comfort in the similar experiences of others. They came to the realization that they were not alone and that many other people had similar concerns. People began to seek strength in unity, realizing that the only way to overcome fear was through collective resilience, which led to the beginnings of the reformation of bonds, albeit on a hesitant basis.

In addition, Sarah and her allies recognized the importance of addressing the structural factors that had contributed to the spread of paranoia in the first place. They worked toward the establishment of systems of transparency and accountability, as well as checks and balances, with the goal of preventing the abuse and manipulation of power. Their determination to construct a society that would never again allow itself to be subjugated by terror was fueled by the lessons that they had learned from the past.

The passage of time resulted in a gradual easing of the hold that paranoia had on the individual. Even though the scars remained, the society had learned to face its fears head-on and to question the narratives that sought to divide and isolate its members. The wounds that were caused by deception served as reminders of the significance of remaining vigilant and the power that comes from coming together.

Sarah recognized the resiliency that resided within each individual as she observed the society that had emerged from the grips of fear. They had been forced to confront their own frailties, and as a result, they had emerged from the experience more powerful and with a renewed commitment to safeguard the well-being of the group. The wounds left by their struggle with paranoia served as a constant reminder of the wars they had fought and the victories they had won.

The road to recovery and reconstruction was only a fraction of the way finished. It would take some time for the wounds caused by fear to completely heal, and the feelings of paranoia would not go away. However, Sarah and her allies did not waiver in their resolve. They were confident that so long as they maintained their cohesiveness, they would be able to surmount any challenge that stood in the way of their common future.

Chapter 16: Redefining Freedom: Defiance in Chains

Sarah Thompson and the other courageous individuals who had fought for justice found themselves confronted with a new challenge as the shattered pieces of their world began to be pieced back together. This new challenge consisted of the task of redefining freedom within the confines of their society. They came to the conclusion that true freedom was not merely the absence of figurative or literal shackles, but rather a mental disposition that called for unyielding defiance in the face of adversity.

A new order had emerged in the wake of the chaos and deception, one that sought to establish control under the guise of stability. This new order had emerged in the wake of the chaos and deception. Dissent was swiftly quelled after the establishment of laws and regulations, as well as the setting of boundaries. It dawned on Sarah and her allies that their battle for freedom was far from over; rather, it had morphed into a conflict to preserve and expand the boundaries of liberty.

They were aware that true freedom entailed more than just the capacity to move and act without hindrance; rather, it encompassed the freedom to think and express oneself, as well as the opportunity to pursue both individual and communal goals. They were aware that the chains of oppression did not need to be tangible in order to exist; rather, they could be intangible and be the result of factors such as fear, conformity, and the silencing of dissent.

Sarah and her allies set out on a mission with the intention of defying these invisible chains and challenging the restrictions that had been placed on their freedom. They organized secret get-togethers in which ideas were discussed, creativity was encouraged, and hopes for a better world were fostered. They refused to be cowed by the oppressive systems that were attempting to stifle their voices, and they refused to let those systems win.

Their defiance was met with retaliation in the form of consequences. In order for the authorities to keep their firm grasp on power, they suppressed any form of opposition and let loose a wave of repression. But Sarah and her allies did not waver in their resolve, as they were well aware that genuine freedom was not without its dangers and that the fight for liberation necessitated making sacrifices.

They organized demonstrations in order to demand accountability and transparency from those in positions of authority. They had the courage to speak out against injustices, shedding light on the shadowy areas in which oppression was still alive and well. They were under the impression that if they questioned the existing order, they would be able to loosen the invisible bonds that held their society together.

As part of their mission to reimagine what it means to be free, Sarah and her allies set out to establish safe havens in which people would feel comfortable revealing their authentic selves without the threat of being judged or punished. They advocated for diversity, understanding that genuine liberty necessitated an openness to the variety of identities, beliefs, and points of view held by its citizens. They dismantled the rigid boundaries that had confined their society for an excessively long time by questioning the accepted norms of society.

However, as they pushed the boundaries of freedom, they met opposition from both inside and outside their own ranks. Some people clung to the stability of the old order out of fear of the unknown and the potential chaos that came along with having their freedom redefined. Others thought their efforts were either naive or dangerous, as they believed that genuine freedom was an ideal that could never be achieved.

Despite this, Sarah and her allies did not waver in their resolve because they had an unshakable faith in the efficacy of defiance. They were well aware that the fight for freedom was an ongoing process, and that it involved a continuous negotiation between individual rights and collective responsibilities. They realized that redefining freedom necessitated striking a delicate balance, one in which the pursuit of personal liberties was inextricably linked to the recognition and observance of the rights of others.

Their unyielding defiance started to pay off in a big way. The germs of their rebellion took root in the minds and hearts of others, which sparked a wave of awakening throughout their society. The invisible chains of fear and conformity were gradually broken, and they were replaced by a spirit of individual empowerment and collective agency.

The society underwent a transformation as the limits of freedom were pushed further and further out. The fullness of the human potential was unlocked, along with its attendant benefits, including the flourishing of creativity and innovation. Those who had long yearned for a world in which individuality was celebrated and dreams were nurtured were drawn to the newly redefined sense of freedom, which became a beacon.

Sarah surveyed the community they had helped mold, a community in which disobedience had been elevated to the status of a virtue and in which the pursuit of freedom was not constrained by chains of any kind, whether they were literal or figurative. The battle for justice had mutated into a conflict for the dignity of the human person, an unrelenting conflict to defend and extend the bounds of personal liberty.

Chapter 17: The Silent Suffering: Tales from the Margins

Sarah Thompson and the resilient souls who had fought for justice turned their attention to the silent suffering that had been ignored for a long time. This included the stories and struggles of those who lived on the margins of society. As the world began to heal and find a new sense of freedom, Sarah Thompson and the others turned their attention to the silent suffering. They understood that genuine liberation included not only their own freedom but also the freedom of all people, irrespective of the conditions in which they were living at the time.

Sarah and her allies went to parts of their world that had been ignored for a long time in an effort to amplify the voices of people whose opinions had been suppressed for an excessive amount of time. They took the time to hear the stories of those who were marginalized, forgotten, and voiceless. They saw the silent suffering that people who were burdened by things like poverty, discrimination, and systemic injustice were forced to endure.

They came to the conclusion that their fight for freedom and justice could not be successful unless they addressed the systemic inequalities that had been plaguing their society from the very beginning. They acknowledged that the newly discovered freedom they had obtained was still a distant dream for many people, as it was overshadowed by the harsh realities of their day-to-day lives.

Sarah and her allies collaborated with grassroots organizations and advocacy groups to address the structural injustices that continued to cause the marginalized population to suffer. This was accomplished by forming alliances with these organizations. They demanded equal access to resources and opportunities for everyone, fought against discrimination, and lobbied for policy reforms.

They did this in order to shed light on the silent suffering that had been hidden away for far too long and to create platforms for those on the margins of society to share their experiences. They wanted to humanize the struggles faced by people living on the margins of society by challenging the perceptions held by society, cultivating empathy and understanding, and using art, literature, and the media to accomplish this goal.

As they dug deeper into the stories from the margins, they came across accounts of people who had overcome adversity, shown strength, and shown courage. They encountered people who, in spite of the difficulties they had to go through, refused to let themselves be defined solely by their situations. In order to break down the barriers that kept marginalized people in the background and to inspire others, Sarah and her allies celebrated these stories and amplified them.

They made efforts to provide concrete support and developed programs to uplift and empower those who were on the margins of society. They provided opportunities for education and skill development, thereby opening up new avenues of possibility. They created secure environments in which people could go to find solace, support, and a feeling that they belonged somewhere. They endeavored to break the cycle of silence by providing those who had been rendered voiceless with a voice of their own.

However, they were aware that their efforts were not sufficient. The marginalized population has historically been subjected to struggles that are deeply ingrained, having their origins in oppressive structures and the prejudices of society. Sarah and her allies understood the importance of bringing about systemic change by removing the obstacles that maintained inequality and hindered individuals' ability to access fundamental rights and resources.

They participated in public discourse, in which they contested the dominant narratives that maintained marginalization and brought attention to the necessity of societal transformation on a more fundamental level. They organized large groups of people, brought awareness to the issue, and demanded accountability from those in positions of power.

As society began to turn its attention toward those who were marginalized, Sarah saw firsthand how the power of collective action and solidarity can move mountains. People from all walks of life joined the fight for justice when they realized that the liberation of society as a whole was inextricably linked to the liberation of those who were on the margins of society.

As the stories that came from the margins became more visible, the society was forced to confront its own complicity in the perpetuation of the silent suffering. The stories that had been ignored for so long became calls to action for reform, which ignited a movement that could no longer be disregarded.

Sarah joined the chorus of people calling for justice, resolute in her mission to give a voice to those who were suffering in silence and to make certain that their plight was not minimized or overlooked. She was aware that in order to achieve true liberation, there needed to be a concerted effort on the part of everyone to bring about the overthrow of oppressive systems and to bring those who were marginalized to a place of dignity, respect, and equal opportunity.

A new chapter in their fight for justice and freedom began to unfold as the world started to acknowledge and address the silent suffering. This chapter embraced the diversity, humanity, and interconnectedness of all individuals. As Sarah and her allies worked toward creating a society in which every person's opinion counted and every life had significance, they were adamant that they would spare no one's story and spare no one's suffering in the process.

Chapter 18: Darkened Hearts: Moral Decay in the Shadows

Sarah Thompson and the remaining members of the resistance discovered a disturbing truth that had been hiding in the shadows. This truth was a moral decay that threatened to erode the very fabric of their society, which occurred as the rest of the world continued to struggle with the aftermath of their turbulent journey. They were forced to deal with the realization that even when people were trying to do the right thing, the human heart could be corrupted and moral standards could be compromised.

The battles of the past had left deep scars, and some people had allowed themselves to be tempted by the promise of power and personal gain as a way to heal those wounds. As Sarah continued her investigation into the core of their society, she came face to face with the repercussions of a deteriorating morality, including avarice, exploitation, and a disregard for the wellbeing of others. The darkness that had once protected them while they fought for freedom now served as a haven for the germinating seeds of evil.

Sarah and her allies did not choose to ignore the moral rot that was spreading throughout their midst. They came to the conclusion that in order to achieve true justice, it was not only necessary to bring down oppressive systems, but also to make an unwavering commitment to upholding the values that had served as the impetus for their resistance.

They made the decision to deal head-on with the evil that existed within their society.

Together, they worked toward rekindling the flame of morality and reminding their fellow citizens of the significance of empathy, compassion, and integrity in their daily lives. They did this by organizing community forums and holding open conversations about the ethical challenges they were up against. They talked about the responsibilities that come with power as well as the impact that individual actions have on the well-being of the group.

Sarah was aware of the fact that moral deterioration was not something that could be repaired overnight. Apathy, complacency, and the gradual deterioration of ethical values were the driving forces behind this gradual process. She was well aware that in order to win the war against immorality, she would need to make a consistent effort toward self-improvement and introspection.

They began educational campaigns that emphasized the significance of making ethical decisions and the repercussions of compromising their morals in any way. They worked toward the establishment of accountability systems, which would hold both individuals and organizations responsible for the consequences of their behaviors. Sarah and the people who supported her believed that if they shed light on the shadowy areas, they could encourage others to rediscover their sense of right and wrong.

But the effort to combat a decline in moral standards was met with opposition. Those people who had given in to the allure of power and personal gain resisted the call to confront their own moral failings even though they knew it was the right thing to do. They were determined to maintain their positions of privilege at any cost, even if it meant taking advantage of the weaknesses of those around them. The fight against moral decay evolved into a conflict with those who had become disoriented and lost their bearings.

THE BLEAK HORIZON: A JOURNEY INTO DARKNESS   71

In their attempt to win back the moral high ground, Sarah and her allies were up against a number of formidable obstacles. As the forces of moral decay fought to maintain their hold on society, they confronted them with deception and manipulation. They knew that their fight was not just for their own liberation; rather, it was for the restoration of the moral compass that had guided them from the very beginning of their journey. Despite this, they did not waiver in their resolve.

They rallied the disillusioned, those who still believed in the efficacy of righteous causes and the fundamental goodness of people everywhere. They banded together in an effort to combat the forces that were contributing to the decline in morality, and they were resolved to bring honor and ethical conduct back to the forefront of their society.

Their actions sent ripples throughout their world as they exposed the people who were responsible for the decline in morality. A collective awakening was sparked as a result of the revelations, as individuals started to question their own decisions and confront the darkness that existed within their hearts. The fight against moral decay turned into an internal struggle for redemption, and it inspired them to recommit themselves to upholding the principles they held most dear.

Sarah and her allies put in a tremendous amount of effort to restore the ethical underpinnings of their society. They celebrated acts of compassion, kindness, and selflessness, making sure that these tales of moral triumph shone brightly even amidst the darkness by highlighting these types of deeds. They were aware that the only way to achieve genuine liberation was to embed moral rectitude into the very fabric of their society before they could consider themselves free.

The tendrils of moral decay began to wither over the course of time, unable to withstand the persistent pursuit of justice and righteousness. Sarah took in their newly remodeled society, one in which moral deterioration was still present but was constantly challenged and kept in check by the concerted efforts of the populace as a whole. Sarah reflected on how their society had evolved.

Chapter 19: Unveiling the Unknown: Secrets of a Broken World

After completing their arduous journey, Sarah Thompson and the other courageous individuals who had fought for justice found themselves up against a new obstacle: a world that was still shrouded in secrets and mysteries. They set out on an adventure with the goal of discovering the unknown and unearthing the secrets that were supposedly buried beneath the surface of their shattered world.

Sarah and her allies were aware that their struggle for justice and freedom could not be won until the lingering shadows and the secrets that had plagued their society for an inordinate amount of time were brought into the light. Sarah and her allies knew that this could not happen until they had confronted the shadows and revealed the secrets. They realized that the information that had been revealed in the past was only the tip of the iceberg, and that in order to experience true healing and transformation, it was necessary for them to gain a deeper understanding of their world.

They combed through long-lost archives, read ancient texts, and sought the counsel of those who had been responsible for the preservation of relics from the past. They pieced together the jigsaw puzzle of their history and followed the threads that had led them to the current state of hopelessness that they were in. The revelations they made were shocking and mind-boggling at the same time; they shed light on the most dismal aspects of their shattered world.

Sarah and her allies were able to uncover hidden agendas, covert experiments, and the abuse of vulnerable people. They came to understand the extent of human greed and the lengths that some people were willing to go to in order to keep their power. They were thrown for a loop by the revelation of the secrets, and the feeling of collective blame and responsibility weighed heavily on all of their hearts.

However, despite being aware of the broken world in which they lived, they refused to let it render them immobile. Instead, they used the information they discovered to act as a driving force behind change. They made a solemn oath to face the darkness head-on, to make certain that the mistakes of the past would not be repeated, and to ensure that the secrets that were buried within their society would be brought into the light of the truth as soon as possible.

Their determination increased as each hidden truth was revealed to them. They began conducting investigations in an effort to bring those who had suffered at the hands of unseen forces a sense of justice. They brought those to justice who were responsible for keeping the secrets and dismantled the systems that had been in place to facilitate their concealment.

The revelation of secrets, as Sarah and her allies came to realize, was not simply about apportioning blame; rather, it was about reclaiming agency and rewriting the narrative of their fractured world. They participated in processes of truth-telling and reconciliation, thereby making room for healing, forgiveness, and redemption to take place. They extended an invitation to the people who had suffered as a result of the secrets for them to tell their stories, to be seen and heard, and to regain their dignity.

The fragmented world started to mend itself as its darkest secrets came to light. The wounds from the past were brought to the surface, but they have since become symbols of the group's progress toward individual and collective healing and transformation. Sarah and her allies forged a new path, one that was directed by transparency, accountability, and a commitment to never forget the lessons that their turbulent history had to teach them.

The revelation of previously hidden information also resulted in the acquisition of fresh knowledge and enlightenment. Sarah and her allies went in search of people who remembered long-lost wisdom and unlocked ancient teachings and forgotten technologies. They unearthed the potential for renewal and regeneration, and they used the power of knowledge that had been lost to rebuild the world that had been destroyed.

Their efforts to discover the truth and expose those responsible for the lies became a beacon of hope for others, motivating them to join their cause. As more people liberated themselves from the shackles of ignorance and apathy and came to the realization that the pursuit of truth was essential for a better future, the momentum gained speed. A shift occurred in the collective consciousness, and the shattered world transformed into a place of rebirth and possibility.

Sarah took in the altered landscape before her, a landscape in which secrets were no longer concealed in the darkness but rather brought into the light with bravery and conviction. The discordant events of their history had given birth to a future that would be constructed on openness, accountability, and an unrelenting search for the truth.

Chapter 20: Reaping the Harvest: Surviving the Barren Land

Following the arduous journey that they had just completed, Sarah Thompson and the other courageous individuals who had fought for justice were confronted with a new obstacle: a desolate land that stretched out in front of them and was devoid of the resources that were required for survival. They set out on a journey to find a harvest in this barren landscape with the intention of finding food and constructing a future for themselves in spite of the daunting odds.

Scars had been left on the land itself as a result of the broken world that they inhabited. The once rich soil has become infertile and unforgiving as a result of environmental degradation, a lack of available resources, and the fallout from previous conflicts. However, Sarah and her supporters refused to give in to hopelessness. They were aware that the only way to thrive despite the challenges that they faced was to devise original solutions.

They conducted research on the land and discovered previously unknown sources of resilience and potential. They rediscovered long-lost information and utilized time-honored methods in order to cultivate crops despite the difficult growing conditions. They discovered, through a process of trial and error, how to modify their agricultural practices by adopting environmentally friendly practices that were compatible with the constraints imposed by the land.

In their struggle to stay alive, Sarah and her allies quickly realized the significance of building a community and working together. They organized themselves into farming collectives in order to increase their chances of being successful by pooling their resources, tools, and expertise. In the face of the unpredictability and difficulty of their environment, they banded together and worked, planting the seeds of hope and resilience in one another.

They did this by tending to a few plots of land with fertile soil and growing crops that were able to survive in the harsh conditions. Each harvest was a victory, serving as a demonstration of their resiliency and unyielding determination. The once desolate land gradually began to produce food, as evidenced by the appearance of various fruits and vegetables where they had previously been absent.

However, in order for them to survive, they relied on more than just agriculture. They began to rely on different resources for sustenance and began to investigate the natural riches that had previously been overlooked. They satiated their hunger by foraging for edible plants, quenching their thirst at natural springs, and powering themselves with sources of renewable energy. They understood that maintaining a delicate balance between humanity and the land was essential to their continued existence, and as a result, they adopted a lifestyle that was sustainable.

While they were gathering the harvest, they also looked into ways that they could restore the land. They adopted practices that promote regeneration, thereby improving the health of the soil and reviving its fertility. They began reforestation projects, during which they planted trees and created microhabitats in order to encourage biodiversity. They realized that their ability to live was dependent on the condition of the land, and as a result, they became stewards responsible for the land's health.

Along the way, Sarah and her allies were met with a number of challenges and obstacles. They had to contend with droughts, infestations of pests, and the ever-present possibility of going hungry. On the other hand, their tenacity and unyielding spirit propelled them forward. They rejoiced over each seemingly insignificant victory, knowing that their very existence depended on their capacity to adjust to their environment and remain resilient.

In the same way that they reaped the harvest from the desolate land, they also reaped the harvest of the fruits of their joint labor. They laid the groundwork for a newfound sense of community and shared purpose by virtue of the bonds they had forged, the lessons they had learned, and the strength they had gained as a result of their experiences. They came to the conclusion that true survival required more than just providing for one's physical needs; it also required tending to one's spirit and learning how to be resilient in the face of adversity.

Sarah saw the desolate land that had been transformed into a place where life had emerged from the void and where the human spirit had triumphed over the most difficult of circumstances. The fact that their small community managed to survive became a symbol of hope for other people, which encouraged resiliency and creativity in the face of limited resources.

Chapter 21: The Bleeding Sky: Nature's Last Stand

S arah Thompson and the other courageous individuals who had fought for justice came face to face with a heartbreaking sight during the final stages of their journey. This sight was a bleeding sky, a poignant symbol of nature's last stand against the advancing darkness. They saw the significant effect that their broken world had on the natural world, which motivated them to take a stand and fight for the preservation of the natural world.

The crimson sky was a jarring visual representation of the ecological devastation that had been inflicted upon their world. The planet had been pushed to its breaking point as a result of unrelenting exploitation of natural resources, widespread pollution, and deforestation. Sarah and her allies were aware that their pursuit of justice and freedom had to go further than the struggles of humans; it also had to include the struggle to restore and preserve the delicate balance that exists in nature.

They embarked on a mission to confront the forces that posed a danger to the very existence of the natural world, which was driven by a profound sense of responsibility on their part. They initiated environmental campaigns with the goals of increasing public awareness of the critical nature of the situation and motivating others to join their cause. They sought alliances with environmental organizations and scientists so that they could combine their respective strengths to advocate for environmentally responsible practices and the preservation of the environment.

When it came to protecting the natural world, Sarah and her allies quickly realized that a comprehensive strategy was necessary. They advocated for stricter regulations and environmentally friendly alternatives while fighting against industries that abused the land and the waterways. They were leaders in the conservation movement, which included establishing protected areas and working to restore ecosystems that had been degraded as a result of human activities.

They also placed an emphasis on education with the goal of instilling in future generations a profound reverence and affection for the natural world. They fostered an appreciation for the natural world's beauty as well as its interconnectedness by organizing nature walks, educational programs, and outreach initiatives. They were under the impression that by cultivating a sense of stewardship, they would be able to bring about a future in which people and nature could coexist peacefully.

However, there were many obstacles to overcome in the effort to save the natural world. The opposition that Sarah and her allies faced came from powerful interests with vested interests in the exploitation of natural resources. They were met with skepticism and apathy from those who put a higher value on immediate profits than on the long-term viability of the venture. The sky was bleeding, which served as a constant reminder of how important it was for them to complete their mission.

They did not give up and instead persisted in recruiting people from a wide variety of backgrounds to support their cause. In order to defend the natural world, they organized demonstrations and direct actions and raised their voices. They appealed to a global audience with their call for environmental justice by leveraging the power of the media and technology to amplify their message and reach a wider audience.

As they carried on with their struggle, they were able to observe the transformative power of collective action. As a result, governments started passing more stringent environmental regulations, businesses started adopting sustainable practices, and individuals started making conscious decisions to lessen the impact they have on the environment. The image of the sky bleeding turned into a rallying cry, sparking a global movement that demanded accountability and action.

Sarah took in the sight of a world that had been altered; a world in which the blood-red sky had been replaced by a sky of brilliant sunsets and clear blue skies. The wounds that had been inflicted upon nature had started to heal, thanks to the efforts of her allies and the collective will of humanity as a whole. Their own search for freedom and justice became entangled with the survival of the natural world and its preservation.

Chapter 22: The Great Divide: Lines Drawn in Blood

Sarah Thompson and the other courageous individuals who had fought for justice found themselves confronted with a new threat after their ceaseless efforts to rebuild and restore their society in the wake of the aftermath of those efforts. This new threat was a growing division within their society that threatened to tear it apart. The progress that they had worked so hard to achieve was in danger of being undone as a result of long-standing disagreements and ideological disparities, which caused people to draw lines in the blood.

Their society was ripped apart by the great divide, which stoked feelings of hostility and mistrust among its members. It led to the formation of factions, each of which was steadfast in their own beliefs and unwilling to compromise. It appeared as though the unity that had once held them together was breaking down, and it was being replaced by hostility and suspicion.

Sarah had the intuitive understanding that their fight for justice and freedom required them to not only prevail over the external forces of oppression they faced, but also to negotiate the complexities that are inherent to human nature. She understood that the wounds of the past had left deep scars that had contributed to the divisions that they were currently experiencing. These divisions, if left unchecked, would render meaningless the hard-fought victories that they have achieved.

Sarah and her allies set out on a journey of dialogue and reconciliation, intent on closing the gap that had been created between the two groups. They organized peace summits in which representatives from competing factions were brought together to have open and honest conversations with one another in an effort to resolve the conflict. They endeavored to gain an understanding of the underlying anxieties, resentments, and hopes that had led to the formation of these divisions in the first place.

They faced the ghosts of the past, acknowledging the suffering and traumatic experiences that had contributed to the formation of their society. They understood that recovery was not a step-by-step procedure but rather a group endeavor that required compassion, empathy, and a readiness to listen. They encouraged forgiveness, knowing that the wounds of the past could not be healed, but that they could be turned into lessons for a better future. They understood that this was the only way to move forward.

In addition, Sarah and the people who supported her understood that in order to bridge the gap, it was necessary to address the structural issues that maintained the conflict. They fought for a more equitable distribution of resources in order to make sure that everyone's requirements were satisfied. They worked to dismantle the systems of oppression and inequality that had fueled the divisions, paving the way for a society in which every voice was heard and valued equally. This was the first step toward creating a society where every voice was heard and valued equally.

However, there was a significant barrier that was difficult to overcome. It was marked by deeply ingrained beliefs, power dynamics that had become ingrained over time, and the scars of past injustices. Those individuals who steadfastly adhered to their ideologies met opposition from Sarah and her allies. These individuals feared that making concessions would water down their identities and lessen the significance of their fights.

Sarah did not give up, despite the obstacles. She was aware of the fact that in order to make genuine progress, it was necessary to locate areas of agreement among the disparities. She actively sought out people who were willing to put aside their differences and come together in the face of adversity, as she understood the value of cohesiveness in such situations. Together, they worked toward the goal of creating places for communication and mutual understanding, erecting bridges where there had previously been only walls.

The path toward bridging the gap was fraught with difficulties at every turn. As old wounds were reopened, it brought about new conflicts, which in turn brought about setbacks and moments of despair. However, Sarah and her allies did not give up the fight. They were steadfast in their commitment to the vision of a unified society in which individuals' unique qualities were embraced and disagreements were resolved through nonviolent means.

Their efforts started to pay off after some time had passed. The lines that had been drawn in blood started to disappear, doing so gradually but inexorably. Individuals, as they participated in meaningful conversations with one another, came to the realization that being divided was pointless and that coming together was powerful. They were able to look past the differences that had previously separated them and recognize the humanity in one another.

Sarah surveyed the society that they had fought so hard to protect; a society in which the great divide had become a testament to the power of understanding and reconciliation as a result of the efforts of everyone involved. Even though the wounds caused by the division were still visible, they served as reminders of the resiliency and compassion that had carried them through the most difficult times.

Chapter 23: A Fractured Identity: Discovering the Truth Within

S arah Thompson and the other courageous individuals who had fought for a better world found themselves confronted with a new challenge as the journey toward justice and freedom unfolded. This new challenge was a fractured identity. They were left wondering who they truly were and what it was that they stood for as a result of the weight of their experiences and the scars that they carried with them. They set out on a quest of introspection, intent on putting their fragmented identities back together and discovering the truth about themselves along the way.

Because of the conflicts they had fought, the sacrifices they had made, and the traumatic experiences they had been through, they now felt disjointed and cut off from their sense of identity as a result. Throughout the course of their journey, they had donned a variety of masks in order to adapt to the ever-shifting environment of their broken world. However, at this point, they yearned for authenticity, wanting to reclaim their true identities and bring those identities into alignment with their core values and beliefs.

In order to investigate the inner workings of their own beings, Sarah and her allies set out on a journey of self-reflection. They actively sought out solitude and opportunities for introspection, using this time to better comprehend how their life experiences had shaped who they were. They faced their anxieties, their uncertainties, and their vulnerabilities head-on, which allowed them to shed the layers of protection they had built up over the years.

They engaged in introspection, posing challenging questions to themselves and allowing themselves to feel the unease that comes with uncertainty. Who were they when they were stripped of the roles they had played during the conflict? What were the fundamental principles that guided their behavior? Beyond the ideologies that they had come to embrace, what did they actually have faith in? They set out to discover the truth that was buried deep within themselves by engaging in extensive introspection.

During Sarah and her allies' process of coming to terms with who they are, they came to realize the significance of community. They were open and honest with one another in their discussions, discussing the challenges and anxieties that they faced on the inside. They found out that they were not the only ones struggling with their fragmented identities and that their fellow soldiers had also faced difficulties of a similar nature. They were able to find the motivation and inspiration to carry on with their mission by drawing upon the collective power of support.

They looked for teachers and wise elders, people who had been down roads leading to self-discovery in a manner comparable to their own. They gained insight and direction from their stories of overcoming adversity and coming to terms with who they were, which served as a source of motivation for them. They understood that the path toward a unified identity was not a linear one, but rather an ongoing process of personal development and awareness of one's surroundings.

They uncovered long-lost truths and came face to face with their own preconceived notions and prejudices as they proceeded deeper into their own interior landscapes. They understood the significance of reconciling with their shadow selves, or the aspects of themselves that they had previously disregarded or repressed. They worked hard to incorporate these aspects of their identities into who they were, knowing that the only way to achieve true wholeness was to accept all aspects of who they were.

As a result of their self-discovery, they started to rethink their identities in terms of their genuineness and the truth about themselves. They discarded the masks and personas that were no longer beneficial to them, and instead embraced their distinct individuality while standing tall in their own vulnerabilities. They came to the conclusion that the fragmentation of their identities was not a sign of weakness but rather an opportunity for personal development and growth.

They were able to reestablish a connection with their purpose and passions as a result of the clarity and acceptance of themselves that had recently come to them. They lived a life that was consistent with their core values and beliefs, which allowed them to bring their outer actions into alignment with their inner truth. They became guiding lights for others to follow, encouraging others to go on their own journeys of self-discovery and accept their fragmented identities as a catalyst for personal and societal change.

Sarah turned her attention to her allies, each of whose faces glowed with the newly discovered radiance of self-realization. Their disjointed identities had become stepping stones on the path to both individual development and the collective empowerment of the group. They had made the journey inward and emerged stronger as a result of their discovery of the truth. They were now united by a shared commitment to authenticity and the pursuit of a better world.

Chapter 24: Lost in the Maze: Navigating the Dystopian Labyrinth

Sarah Thompson and the courageous individuals who had fought for justice found themselves confronted with a complex maze of difficulties and obstacles as they continued their journey through the dystopian landscape. They lived in a dystopian world that was a labyrinth of convoluted systems, structures that repressed people, and threats that were concealed. They were struggling to find their way out of the maze-like environment in which they found themselves, which was filled with perilous pathways.

The maze appeared to be designed with the express purpose of confusing, disorienting, and entrapping them. As a result of the use of deception, propaganda, and manipulation in the construction of the walls of the labyrinth, both the truth and reality have been distorted. Every one of their advances was met with resistance from adversaries who were adamant about preserving the status quo. This made every one of their steps forward feel like a test.

In order to find their way through the labyrinth, Sarah and her allies had to rely on their resourcefulness, resilience, and collective wisdom. They conducted an investigation of the patterns, dissected the narratives, and looked for different points of view. They were aware that in order to find a way out of the labyrinth, they needed to investigate the structure's fundamental underpinnings and principles.

They searched for the truth amidst a sea of lies, peeling back the layers of propaganda that had been used to manipulate the general population. They challenged the narratives that were imposed upon them and sought independent sources of information. They engaged in critical thinking. They came to the conclusion that the only way for them to be set free was to disentangle themselves from the web of manipulation and reclaim authority over their own ideas and convictions.

During the course of their travels through the dystopian labyrinth, they ran into a number of physical obstacles. Checkpoints, surveillance networks, and fortified structures were all deployed with the intention of restricting their freedom and controlling their movements. But Sarah and her allies were resolute in their pursuit to triumph over these challenges. They worked hard to improve their abilities, coming up with clever plans to circumvent safety precautions and gain an advantage over their opponents.

They discovered comfort and direction in the accounts of those who had traversed the labyrinth before them, whose experiences provided them with both. They unearthed previously unknown networks of resistance and established connections with individuals and communities that had successfully defied the authoritarian systems. They collaborated on an underground network of support and solidarity by exchanging information, methods, and instruments of all kinds.

They were forced to confront their own personal demons as they progressed further into the labyrinth. The maze had a way of putting their fortitude to the test, driving them to their breaking point, and luring them into making sacrifices to their principles. They faced their anxieties, their uncertainties, and the shadow side that existed within themselves. They were able to find the resilience necessary to keep going when they stopped to think about themselves and draw on their inner strength.

In the end, Sarah and her allies came to the conclusion that they could not successfully navigate the labyrinth on their own. They connected with other people and organizations that had a similar outlook on how the world should be and worked to form coalitions and alliances with them. They understood the importance of working together and the benefits that accrued from maintaining a unified front in the face of challenges.

They never lost sight of their ultimate goal, which was to find a way out of the dystopian labyrinth and create a new reality that was based on justice, freedom, and equality, despite the difficulties and setbacks they encountered. They never allowed themselves to become complacent or resigned to the confines of the maze, and as a result, they were able to persevere.

They were gaining a deeper understanding of the labyrinth as well as the systems that kept it alive with each step that they took forward. They discovered its vulnerabilities and began chipping away at the oppressive structures that were holding them captive. They uncovered previously unknown passageways, which allowed them to create alternate routes that posed a threat to the labyrinth's authority.

Sarah turned her attention to her allies, whose eyes revealed a steely resolve despite the obvious signs of exhaustion. They had not given up hope despite the fact that they were lost in the dystopian labyrinth. They were aware that with each turn and twist, they were getting one step closer to figuring out how to get out of the maze and into the light of a new dawn.

Chapter 25: The Silent Scream: Voices of the Oppressed

Sarah Thompson and the other courageous individuals who had fought for justice heard the muffled screams of those who were oppressed reverberating through the shadows of their broken society. They were located deep within the dystopian world. They set out on a mission to amplify these voices and to provide a platform for those whose cries had been muted for a significantly longer period of time than was acceptable.

The oppressed people had their humanity and dignity taken away from them, and they were reduced to nothing more than numbers and statistics in the apparatus of oppression. The oppressed people's voices needed to be heard, acknowledged, and valued, and Sarah and her allies were aware of the critical necessity of breaking the chains of silence that were keeping them silent.

They went deep into the heart of the communities that were oppressed, into the forgotten corners where the people who lived there were hidden. They listened to their accounts, becoming witnesses to the suffering, pain, and resiliency that lay beneath the surface. They were aware of the fact that genuine liberation could not be attained until the voices of the oppressed were provided with a forum in which they could be heard.

These voices were amplified through the use of platforms that Sarah and her allies possessed. They made it possible for those who had been oppressed to tell their stories without fear of being judged or ridiculed in the process. They took advantage of the power of the media, art, and technology to disseminate these narratives to a wide audience, thereby shedding light on the harsh realities that are experienced by those who are marginalized.

They demanded justice and equality by participating in demonstrations and rallies, marching in solidarity with those who were being oppressed. They banded together with various advocacy groups and grassroots organizations, and by doing so, they were able to magnify the impact that they had collectively. They demanded accountability and change from the oppressive systems that maintained a culture of silence, which they challenged.

As a result of their efforts, the repressed cries of those who were oppressed started to become audible throughout society. Their narratives reawakened empathy and roused the consciousness of those who had previously chosen to look the other way. It was no longer possible to disregard or ignore the cries of those who were being oppressed. The voices that had been suppressed for such a significant amount of time grew increasingly louder and demanded to be heard.

It was clear to Sarah and the other allies she had that simply giving a voice to those who were being oppressed was not enough. They labored tirelessly to bring down the oppressive structures that, in the first place, had served to stifle these voices' ability to be heard. They fought against inequality, discrimination, and abuses of power in society. They advocated for structural changes and pushed for policy reforms that would make society more just and equitable. They were successful in both of these endeavors.

They ran into opposition from people who wanted to keep things the way they were while they were trying to do the right thing and seek justice. The oppressive forces retaliated, making an effort to stifle the voices that they had previously worked so hard to suppress. But Sarah and her allies held their ground and refused to back down from their position. They understood that the power of the voices of those who were being oppressed was greater than the power that the oppressor possessed.

The uprising of the oppressed as a group eventually became a formidable adversary over the course of history. Their accounts motivated many individuals to become involved in the struggle for justice, which resulted in a groundswell of support and solidarity. The walls of silence started to fall apart, and they were soon replaced by a chorus of voices demanding change, equity, and the recognition of the inherent worth of every individual.

When Sarah looked out over the changed landscape, she saw a society in which the screams of silence had been replaced by a symphony of resilience and resistance. The oppressed had finally found a way to express themselves, and the tales they told became the rallying cry for a more promising future. The path toward genuine liberation became more transparent than it had ever been as a result of the amplification of these voices.

Chapter 26: Embers of Redemption: Rekindling the Human Spirit

After the dystopian upheaval, Sarah Thompson and the other courageous individuals who had fought for justice shifted their focus to rekindling the human spirit and igniting the embers of redemption within themselves and within their society. They realized that removing oppressive systems was not enough to achieve true liberation; rather, it required a widespread awakening of the human spirit as well as the restoration of compassion, empathy, and connection among people.

Sarah and her allies decided to embark on a journey of personal and collective transformation when they came to the realization that the first step toward mending their fractured world was to mend the individuals who lived in it. They engaged in activities that fostered introspection and care for the self, thereby nourishing their own souls and tending to the wounds that had been caused by the conflict. They sought forgiveness and accepted their own shortcomings, fully aware that in order to be redeemed, they needed to have compassion for themselves and be willing to develop.

They reached out to those who were struggling and offered assistance as part of their charitable and community service activities. They were aware that the only way to achieve redemption was through actions that originated from a place of empathy and comprehension. They cultivated an environment of care and support by providing individuals with spaces in which they could find solace, healing, and a feeling of belonging.

Sarah and her allies were aware of the power that can be harnessed through the art of storytelling in order to rekindle the spirit of the human race. They shared their own experiences of adversity and growth, which encouraged others to set out on their own paths to redemption. They elevated the stories of resiliency, forgiveness, and personal growth in order to weave a collective narrative that celebrated the inherent worth and potential that is present within each individual.

They participated in practices of restorative justice, which offered opportunities for healing and reconciliation to those who had been wronged in the past, including the victims as well as the perpetrators. They established platforms for conversation, which gave people the opportunity to admit the wrongdoing that had been done and look for ways to make amends. They understood that in order to be redeemed, they needed to take responsibility for their actions and make a commitment to mending the fabric of their society.

In order to rekindle the human spirit, Sarah and her allies were also aware of the power that connection possessed. They encouraged people from different backgrounds to come together and find things that they had in common by creating spaces for dialogue and collaboration and facilitating those spaces. They rejoiced in the bounty of diversity, fully aware that it was only through the acceptance of one another's unique qualities that true redemption and harmony could be attained.

They did this by investing in education and mentorship programs that instilled values such as empathy, compassion, and social responsibility in the next generation. They realized that the youth needed to be actively engaged and given agency in order for the human spirit to be rekindled. This was because the youth held the potential to shape a future that was built on redemption and a profound sense of humanity.

There was a discernible shift that took place as the embers of redemption began to glow within people's hearts and throughout society. As more people became aware of their interconnectedness and the effect their actions had on those around them, the number of acts of kindness and compassion also increased. On their path toward redemption as a group, the virtues of empathy, forgiveness, and self-improvement emerged as the guiding principles.

Sarah took in the altered landscape before her, one in which the fire of the human spirit had been reignited and redemption had evolved into a community-wide mission. Even though the wounds of the past were not forgotten, they now served as reminders of the transformative power of compassion, forgiveness, and personal development. As a result of Sarah and her allies' dedication to redeeming their past mistakes, a spark of hope was ignited, which shed light on the way forward toward a more favorable future.

Chapter 27: Frayed Bonds: Love and Loss in the Wreckage

Sarah Thompson and the other brave souls who had fought for justice in the aftermath of the dystopian chaos found themselves struggling with the frayed bonds of love and the overwhelming weight of loss in the wreckage of their broken world. They traveled through a landscape of broken relationships while lamenting what they had lost and searching for solace amidst the ruins of their lives.

They had embarked on a journey that had a significant impact on their personal lives, and it had not been easy. There was strain put on familial ties, friendships fell apart, and romantic relationships were put through their paces to the breaking point. Deep scars were left on their hearts as a result of the hurt caused by betrayal, separation, and sacrifice. As they tried to make sense of their severed connections, they struggled under the weight of love and loss that they carried with them.

In the midst of the devastation, Sarah and her allies came to the realization that it was necessary to face the pain head-on and seek healing. They established gathering places for communal mourning and grieving, places where individuals could freely express their sadness and share their experiences of love and bereavement with one another. They held memorial services as a way of paying respect to the people whose lives and relationships had been irrevocably altered as a result of the perilous journey.

They provided support and comfort to one another by leaning on one another, offering a shoulder to cry on and an understanding ear. They were aware that being vulnerable and being willing to acknowledge and be present for one another's suffering were prerequisites for the healing process. They reminded one another that they were not the only ones going through the challenges that they were facing, and they wove a safety net of compassion and understanding for one another.

They learned the value of community and the importance of choosing one another as family in the midst of the devastation. They found comfort in one another's shared experiences of loss and a common desire to rebuild their lives, which led to the formation of new connections and the strengthening of existing ones. Even in the midst of the devastation, they maintained the conviction that love had the potential to serve as a wellspring of fortitude and resiliency.

Sarah and her allies all had their own personal struggles going on inside of them. They reflected on the decisions that they had made, the sacrifices that they had made, and the toll that it had taken on their personal lives as a result of the choices that they had made. They struggled with feelings of guilt and regret, as well as a sense of alienation from the people who had been dear to them in the past. They started their journey toward personal healing and reconciliation by engaging in some self-reflection and forgiving themselves.

They worked toward redefining their relationships, with the goals of fostering open communication and reestablishing trust. They acknowledged the anguish and suffering that had been caused by one another in the course of their heartfelt conversations. They were willing to forgive one another and eagerly embraced the opportunity for personal development and change. They were aware that the bonds of love, despite being frayed, had the potential to be mended and strengthened through the application of intentional effort and the willingness to be vulnerable.

They came to realize that the human capacity for resiliency and healing was limitless as they navigated the complexities of love and loss. They discovered glimmers of happiness in the midst of their suffering, laughter in the midst of their tears, and hope in the midst of their despair. They became adept at keeping the recollections of their departed loved ones close to their hearts, thereby perpetuating the legacies of those individuals even as they worked to reconstruct their lives.

Sarah turned her attention to her allies, each of whose faces bore the marks left by the experiences they had been through in their own lives. They had come to terms with the bittersweet nature of love and loss, realizing that the extent of their suffering was a reflection of the extent to which they were able to love. As a result, they had learned to embrace this nature. They discovered, as a result of their collective resiliency, that even in the midst of the destruction, bonds could be repaired, and new connections could be established.

Chapter 28: The Dark Harvest: Sacrifices for Survival

Sarah Thompson and the other brave souls who had fought for justice found themselves confronted with the harsh reality of the sacrifices that had to be made for the sake of survival as the fight for survival continued in their dystopian world. They struggled with the ethical implications of their decisions while simultaneously weighing the consequences of their actions against the pressing requirement to maintain their lives.

The dystopian environment required sacrifices to be made on a number of different fronts. They had to contend with a lack of resources, a restricted supply of food and clean water, and the ever-present risk of being ambushed by an adversary who hid in the shadows. The decisions that they made had significant repercussions not only for their own lives but also for the lives of those who were close to them.

Sarah and her allies were aware that there was frequently a cost associated with surviving. They chose to forego their own wants and comforts in order to put the needs of the community ahead of their own in order to make difficult decisions. They did things like ration the food they had, share the few resources they had, and come up with plans to reduce the dangers they faced. They were aware that the group's survival depended on their sacrifices, and they were willing to make those sacrifices.

They not only had to contend with the harsh realities of their world, but they also had to wrestle with moral conundrums. They were put in a position where they had no choice but to navigate the murky waters between doing the right thing and doing the wrong thing as a result of the desperate decisions they were forced to make. They questioned the ethics of what they were doing and sought solace in the belief that the sacrifices they were making would pave the way for a brighter future.

In the course of their fight for survival, they were witnesses to acts of heroism and selflessness that shone like a beacon of light in the midst of the darkness. There are some people who are willing to put their lives in danger to save the lives of others, thereby putting their own safety second to the welfare of the community in which they live. These courageous deeds and selfless acts served as an example of the resiliency of the human spirit while also serving as a source of motivation.

Sarah and her allies were aware of the toll that these sacrifices took on their mental and emotional well-being, and they acknowledged this fact. Grief, survivor's guilt, and the burden of carrying the weight of responsibility for the lives of their loved ones were all challenges that they had to face. They provided support for one another by leaning on one another, offering a shoulder to cry on and an ear to listen. They were able to find solace in the collective healing process by recognizing the pain that they carried and by showing compassion and understanding to one another.

They persevered through the challenges and difficulties by clinging to the conviction that their efforts would not be in vain. They maintained an attitude of optimism because they were confident that the efforts they made in the here and now would pave the way for a better life in the future. They centered their efforts on developing resiliency, not only for themselves but also for the generations that would come after them.

Sarah took a look around at her allies, each of whom bore the scars of determination and self-sacrifice on their faces. They had been forced to make decisions that put their humanity and resiliency to the test, and as a result, they had been confronted with the harsh realities of their world. They had established a connection with one another that was unaffected by the gloom, and it served as a constant reminder of the resilience they possessed in the face of adversity because of the sacrifices they had made.

Chapter 29: The Bleak Horizon: Confronting the Final Frontier

Sarah Thompson and the other brave souls who had fought for justice stood on the edge of the desolate horizon as they neared the end of their journey. This was the final frontier that held the promise of a fresh start. They were about to face the toughest challenge they had ever encountered as they got ready to face the unknowable and determine the fate of their shattered world.

The desolate horizon served as a visual representation of the vast expanse of unpredictability that lay in wait for them. It was a symbol of the remnants of a society that had fallen apart and the burden of the past that continued to linger. Sarah and her allies were well aware that in order to make progress, they would need to face the demons of their past and break free from the shackles of the dystopian world that had imprisoned them for such a significant amount of time.

They set out on an adventure into the unknown with a resolve in their hearts, determined to see what lay ahead of them. They confronted the survivors of the repressive regime and tore down the remaining structures that maintained power and control. They confronted the legacy of fear and injustice and worked tirelessly to bring about truth, reconciliation, and transformation in the world.

As they proceeded further into the desolate horizon, they came across pockets of resistance and hidden enclaves that had managed to keep a glimmer of hope despite the oppression and gloom that surrounded them. They established coalitions, bringing together previously separate groups and bringing them together under a shared goal of achieving a more favorable future. They were well aware that the upcoming challenges would require them to rely heavily on their combined resources in order to be successful.

Sarah and her allies worked toward the goal of reestablishing the foundations of their society based on the principles of freedom, equality, and justice. They put in place procedures that made everyone's health and happiness a top priority, and as a result, nobody was left behind. They participated in restorative practices, with the goal of mending the wounds that had been caused by the past and creating an atmosphere that was characterized by empathy, compassion, and comprehension.

They turned to scientific research and creative endeavors as means to influence the course of the future. They did this by harnessing alternative sources of energy, developing environmentally friendly technologies, and looking for ways to reduce the environmental damage that had been done to their world. They recognized that their survival was intricately intertwined with the health of the planet, and as a result, they adopted a relationship with nature that was peaceful and harmonious.

They not only faced the final frontier, but also the depths of their own inner selves as they moved forward in their journey. They set out on a quest of self-discovery with the intention of shedding the remnants of their former identities and embracing the individuals they had evolved into. They faced their anxieties and uncertainties head on, discovering their strength in being vulnerable and accepting themselves.

The hopeless outlook on the horizon was gradually replaced with a blank canvas of opportunities as a result of their combined efforts. They reestablished their society based on the principles of cooperation, equity, and openness to others' perspectives. They recognized that true progress could only be accomplished through unity and a shared purpose, and they celebrated the fact that there was a wide variety of voices and points of view.

Sarah looked out over the new horizon and saw a place where the scars of the past had been transformed into the seeds of a compassionate and resilient society. The journey that they had set out on had been arduous, and it had been full of challenges, sacrifices, and difficulties. However, by maintaining unyielding determination and a strong sense of community, they were successful in establishing a fresh start.

Chapter 30: A Glimpse of Dawn: Embracing the Unknown Future

Sarah Thompson and the other brave souls who had fought for justice stood at the threshold of a new era as the sun began to rise on the horizon. They had been fighting for justice. The journey that they had set out on had led them to this critical juncture—a glimpse of dawn, where the opportunities of an unknowable future beckoned to them.

They embraced the unpredictability of the future with optimism in their hearts and the wisdom gained from the challenges they had overcome in the past. They were aware that their journey was not yet finished and that the way that lay ahead of them would continue to be fraught with difficulties and difficulties. They were fueled by the belief that a better world was within reach, which gave them the determination to face these challenges head-on.

The spirit of resilience that had carried Sarah and her allies through the most difficult times was embraced by Sarah and her allies. They were well aware that in order to succeed in the future, they would need to be adaptable, creative, and willing to learn from their past mistakes. They did not close themselves off to novel concepts and points of view, realizing that the breadth of their life experiences would be their most valuable resource in the process of fashioning a future that would do justice to the principles they held most dear.

They understood that the challenges they were up against could only be overcome through collective effort, so they worked to foster an environment that encouraged collaboration and cooperation. They fostered innovation and developed the skills and interests of individuals, giving those individuals the ability to contribute their one-of-a-kind set of knowledge and abilities to the overall effort of creating a better future for everyone.

The next generation was something that Sarah and her allies looked to with a sense of responsibility as well as hope. They made investments in education and programs that paired mentors with students, making certain that the life lessons they had gained would be passed down to subsequent generations. They did this because they were aware that young people held the key to creating a sustainable and just society, so they fostered the youth's curiosity, creativity, and compassion.

As they moved forward into the unknown, they maintained their vigilance and remained committed to safeguarding the difficultly earned progress that they had achieved. They were aware that the germs of oppression and injustice were still present in the background, waiting to sprout if nobody paid attention to them for a while. They stood as defenders of liberty, constantly on the lookout for any indications of backsliding and steadfastly committed to ensuring that the lessons that were learned in the past would not be forgotten.

On their journey, Sarah and her allies made sure to celebrate each victory, no matter how large or how small. They took great pleasure in the times of happiness, love, and connection that had enabled them to persevere through the most trying of circumstances. They realized that it was essential to find moments of celebration and gratitude, even in the face of adversity, because these moments provided the fuel to keep moving forward in spite of the challenges they were facing.

They had their sights set on a time and place in the future that was unknown, and they welcomed the uncertainty as an opportunity for personal development and change. They took on each new obstacle with bravery and resiliency, knowing that they had the power to determine their own course in life and how it would play out. Their unwavering faith in justice, equality, and the inherent worth of each individual served as the compass that directed their actions.

Sarah turned her attention to the faces of her allies and saw that they were brimming with resolve and optimism. They had traveled so far, through a path filled with gloom and despondency, to arrive at this point, where they stood on the brink of an uncharted future. They had come out on the other side of the storms even stronger, united by a common goal and a sense of community spirit.

They took a step forward as a unit, ready to face the unknown with both their hearts and minds wide open. The journey was not over, but as they ventured into the uncharted territory of the future, they knew that they carried with them the lessons and the resiliency that would guide them towards a world where justice, freedom, and compassion reigned supreme. The journey had not yet ended.

Also by Declan Hunter

About the Publisher

Accepting manuscripts in the most categories. We love to help people get their words available to the world.

Revival Waves of Glory focus is to provide more options to be published. We do traditional paperbacks, hardcovers, audio books and ebooks all over the world. A traditional royalty-based publisher that offers self-publishing options, Revival Waves provides a very author friendly and transparent publishing process, with President Bill Vincent involved in the full process of your book. Send us your manuscript and we will contact you as soon as possible.

Contact: Bill Vincent at rwgpublishing@yahoo.com